The Uninvited Guest

The

Uninvited Guest

A Novel

JOHN DEGEN

NIGHTWOOD EDITIONS
ROBERTS CREEK, BC
2006

Published by Nightwood Editions

R.R. #22, 3692 Beach Ave.
Roberts Creek, BC, Canada V0N 2W2
www.nightwoodeditions.com

Edited by Silas White
Cover photo: Katie West, www.katiewest.ca
Author photo by Julia Colyar

Typeset in Minion and Bodoni
Printed and bound in Canada

Nightwood Editions acknowledges financial support from the Government
of Canada through the Canada Council for the Arts and the Book Pub-
lishing Industry Development Program (BPIDP), and from the Province of
British Columbia through the British Columbia Arts Council, for its pub-
lishing activities.

LIBRARY AND ARCHIVES CANADA CATALOGUING IN PUBLICATION

Degen, John

   The uninvited guest / John Degen.

ISBN 0-88971-216-6

   I. Title.

PS8557.E368U58 2006   C813'.6   C2006-901488-4

for all the Nicolaes

He holds him with his skinny hand,
'There was a ship,' quoth he.
'Hold off! unhand me, grey-beard loon!'
Eftsoons his hand dropt he.

He holds him with his glittering eye—
The Wedding-Guest stood still,
And listens like a three years' child:
The Mariner hath his will.

The Wedding-Guest sat on a stone:
He cannot choose but hear;
And thus spake on that ancient man,
The bright-eyed Mariner.

—Samuel Taylor Coleridge,
"The Rime of the Ancient Mariner"

When you are playing for the national championship, it's not
a matter of life or death. It's more important than that.

—Duffy Daugherty, coach of Michigan State University's
football team between 1954 and 1972. As a player at
Syracuse University in 1938, Daugherty broke his neck on the field,
and played the rest of the season wearing a protective collar.

In Montreal, on a summer evening, a young man named Tony sits with a dead man named Stan in a room growing slowly darker as the day finishes itself outside the windows. The air of the city is breezy and warm, inviting. The room is clean and decorated so as not to offend. It contains several chairs, a small couch, some tables for flowers, and a casket on a skirted, wheeled trolley. There is a distant hiss of air conditioning.

Tony is waiting to be asked to leave. He knows Stan. He's worked with him for a number of years, has drunk beer by his side on bar stools in this very city.

Tony wonders about his duty to stay in the room with the corpse of his friend. He'd like to ask someone what he should do. He'd like to ask Stan, since Stan always seemed to know what to do in these situations, always had a reasonable plan for getting the job done. There is a driver waiting outside, and there is the question of storage. There is no one to ask. The funeral director had told Tony he could wait in this room, but he isn't sure if that means he *must* wait in this room. He waits for the funeral director to return and tell him to leave.

"Stan," Tony says, surprising himself. "Stan, what should I do here? You're dead, after all, and I haven't eaten anything all day. I'm tired Stan, and we have a long drive ahead of us tomorrow."

The dead man says nothing.

"It doesn't feel right leaving you here like this, Stan," Tony continues, feeling again the weight of the situation, the solitude of being someone in charge of a dead man.

"If you were alive, you know, we'd make a night of it—any way you'd like. We could do the bars if you wanted, or just play cards in the room. But this is a whole different situation now. I've got to call the League, Stan. I've got to report that I have you stored away safely, and the Cup, you know. They'll want to know."

He takes a turn around the room. Through the window he watches the taxis on Ontario Street. It's a Thursday evening, and all the cabs contain young people, people Tony's age dressed for the clubs and no doubt smelling nice. He catches a face in each cab going by, a smiling, laughing face, a face telling the story of the evening to come. There are ivies on the windowsill. He sees now they are not plastic as he'd assumed, but real and climbing in behind the heavy curtains and up the latticed panes. All living things want out of this room, Tony thinks.

"I think everyone out there is going to get laid tonight, Stan. I think they're all on their way."

A small table by the door holds the guest book with his solitary name inscribed on the top line of the first page. There had been no need to sign it. He'd seen the weary look of impatience on the funeral director's face as he scratched his name on the page. No one else would visit, and tomorrow Stan would be on his way back to Toronto to be buried alone in a plot paid for by the League. Still, Tony had seen the empty book on his way in. He'd stopped and signed it with the pen on the chain. Now, in the table's one drawer he finds four identical guest books, all empty, and nine new pens waiting to be attached to chains. He signs each book on the top line of the first page and returns them to their hiding place in the drawer.

"I wish I was getting laid tonight, Stan," Tony says. "Tonight especially. Something about being here with you makes a man want to be with a woman. No offence."

Something will have to be decided soon. He knows the driver is becoming impatient outside. He's sure the funeral director is somewhere in the building, waiting for him to leave, perhaps even watching him pace the room on some hidden camera. Tony knows at some point soon he will have to leave this room, leave Stan to wait out the first night of his death alone. "Stan, did I ever tell you the story of my middle name? You know the middle name is the one that contains the secrets. Did I ever tell you about mine? Probably. Let me tell you again."

One

L ate in the season of 1951, Stan Cooper kept time at the arena in Toronto. Seated behind glass at the centre line, he watched the game peripherally, seeing only the referee and linesmen. The sound of a whistle was electric to him, and he responded by flicking the switch to cut the clock. He worked the rhythms of a game, feeling for the next shrill sound. If the action went past three minutes uninterrupted he felt it in his chest as a growing tension. The puck skipped over the glass, a goalie covered up, exhausted wingers fell in the corners. Stan's finger hummed in the half-second before the whistle. He prompted air from the lungs of three men in striped shirts. He willed everyone in the building to exhale and get ready for more.

His job required a colour-blindness, an inability to discern between flying shapes moving in and around the officials. For Stan, it required that he did not read the sports sections of newspapers and that he respond with the same nervous laugh to every half-begun conversation about hockey. The things he could not ignore—the weight of crowd noise in response to a team's relative success or failure, the length of his working season (longer in playoff years), the buzz of traffic around Yonge and Carlton streets on Fridays, Saturdays and some mid-week evenings—these things that revealed the obvious to him, that his home team had a shot, that he might work the finals, he banished these things as best he could. Teams win championships, clocks tell time. Two separate and joined realities, but he had control over only one of them. He played time, and the game was his own. Black or white, binary, absolute. It ran or it stopped. He did not even watch the puck when it dropped for a faceoff. He watched the muscles of the official's hand. It was the absence of a puck that set time moving again. A hand, suddenly empty.

Moving home through traffic, down Church Street to Queen and then out across the Don River Valley into lower Riverdale, he did not actually know who had won. The density of the air in the building at the moment of the final whistle would have told him enough, but he prided himself on not knowing the score. The referee controlled the score, while he just changed the numbers and then forgot what they meant. The hockey he actually watched was at home on Saulter Street where the raised CN tracks slanted across the roadway, cutting his whole neighbourhood off from the long flat approach to Lake Ontario.

In the impromptu cul-de-sac, kids came out nightly to run around passing and shooting old rubber balls. These games were untimed even by the sun, the shouts of children lasting well past any reasonable limitation imposed by darkness. On evenings he was home, Stan watched them from his front step, happily off the clock. And when it was obviously becoming too late to play, when mothers were starting to glance out windows, it was always "next goal wins." Next goal wins, no matter the actual score—plunk that ball in the back of the net and it's over. These kids didn't care enough about their skills, didn't feel their losses deeply enough to generate anything near the passion needed to get off the streets and onto skates in a professional arena. They were losers, and Stan loved watching losers play hockey. To him, it was the only pure form of the sport.

Toronto won the 1951 championship over Montreal in five games. To win a series in five indicates, if not a rout, certainly a singular dominance, the losing team managing to scratch out but one win in the entire series. A five-game series is a worse embarrassment for the losing team than a four-game sweep, because the lack of a sweep indicates there were flaws in the winning team, there were weaknesses to be exploited but your team didn't exploit them. You had them all figured out for one game, but then you forgot what you had learned. They didn't win; you lost. The last game Stan Cooper ever worked as official timekeeper was the third game of the 1951 finals.

The first two games of the series were played in Montreal, at the Forum on Sainte-Catherine Street. The Toronto team sickened all of Quebec with a surprise first-game victory. Montreal had beaten the powerful and favoured Detroit team four games to two in the semifinals, and was expected to win handily over an unfocused Toronto squad. But Toronto outworked and outhit their rivals, sending three players out of the game with injuries in the first period alone. That night, the visiting players were locked into their hotel by their head coach, Joe Primeau. They ate from room service and Primeau stood in the kitchen to watch it being prepared. A crowd of Montrealers gathered outside the hotel, shouting insults and burning blue and white sweaters in the streets.

Montreal's only win in that championship series came the next night. Stan didn't listen to the away games. He avoided all mention of how the team was doing in preparation for the three games he was to work at the arena. But there was no shouting on Queen Street late that night. No banging of pots on the front porches of his neighbourhood. He knew they had lost game two and that the series was tied. He worked in his garden that night, planting peas and tomatoes, and building a scaffold of wooden stakes for his beans to climb. A few minutes past ten, he chased a raccoon from his back shed. The moon was full, or he might have stepped on his rake and clobbered himself. Inside the house, his wife talked on the telephone. He stopped occasionally and listened for words, hearing "blue" and "Penetang" and "bristles."

Game three cost Stan his job and a faith in things as they seem. Game three was fifty-nine minutes and fifty-seven seconds of business as usual for the clock-watcher and five seconds of timekeeping insanity. Game three was the end of Stan's ten-year, childless marriage. The beginning of his irrational hatred for all things tartan. Game three finished Montreal at a spiritual level, broke their shins and left them shaking their heads and crying on the ice.

Montreal tied the score at two goals apiece at 19:27 of the final period. Before that goal, the air in the Gardens was sweetened with screaming voices and the discarded wrappings of thousands of ice cream sandwiches. At 19:25 the ice gleamed in that way that let Stan know he would be going home soon. Blue and white sweaters passed by him like darts while red sweaters drifted, collided, slammed into the glass. At 19:26 a stick blade hit the ice and shattered, sending both puck and wooden fragments toward the goal. At 19:27 the building lost its voice. The goalie had blocked the stick blade and let the puck slip under his arm. The red sweaters danced and Stan went through his time board checklist: minutes, seconds, home goals, visiting goals, period, penalty time. Minutes, seconds, home goals, visiting goals, period, penalty time.

More whistles blew and the black and white sweaters raced into a corner to break up a fight. The game might go into overtime. It could be a long night. The raccoons might get to his young tomato plants. He ran through the checklist and glanced at his wife's seat. He looked at the seats he had given to his wife and his friend James Cole. They were easy to spot because Jim was wearing his ridiculous yellow plaid cap.

Stan had not looked from his scoreboard to the crowd in four years. He ran through the checklist. They were eating ice cream sandwiches, and smiling. His wife used her long nails to pull away the waxed paper from Jim's disintegrating sandwich. Gold seats, on the aisle, for the two people he preferred among all people, save his mother who was no longer alive. He ran through the checklist and waited for the whistle, his finger on the switch. She laughed and wiped ice cream from the corner of her mouth with a paper napkin.

At 19:57 a whistle blew and all the sweaters glided back to the Montreal end to restart after the puck had been iced. The sweaters moved slowly, tired, saving whatever was left for overtime. The building was loud again. People banged

on the glass as the sweaters passed. They were angry for
resolution. They wanted it over. Stan let his eyes rise to his
wife, her hand on Jim's right knee, her nails clutching at the
blue and white checked trousers in nervous anticipation.
The sweaters stopped moving, and Jim's hand landed on
top of hers, softly, like it knew how to be there.

There was movement in the corner of his eye, a reflection on the far glass across the arena. Stan turned his head
to the turmoil on the ice and at the same time pressed the
button to start the clock, fully two seconds too late. At
19:59, the puck slipped across the line beneath a desperately
outstretched glove and game three was over. The winning
goal was scored one full second after the end of the third
period.

Even in the empty cave of the crowd's celebration, Stan
understood he was not the only one who knew. The result
stood, with deep resentment and complaint from the Montreal bench. The next night, Stan watched game four from
the retired player's box high above the north seats. Bill Barilko's heroics in game five carried the controversy of Stan's
two-second blunder out of the papers. The disappearance
of the young defender during a fishing trip that summer
buried it forever. The 1951 finals, which could easily have
been known as the Stan Cooper finals, instead went to the
body of Barilko, lost on the bottom of some northern lake.

Two

"You know that guy who gets knocked flat at the blue line because he's looking at his skates instead of watching the forechecker—the guy who finds himself pleased to remember his own name about ten minutes later while the team doctor is stitching parts of his face? That was me."

Stan and Tony sat side by side at the bar of the Moose Lodge in Kingston, Ontario. Behind them, a party picked up steam. Some young man, a hero in this town, had won all there was to win in hockey, and Stan and Tony, employees of the game, were being paid to keep track of the hoopla. It was rare for Tony to accompany Stan on one of his business trips. Usually he took care of things back at the office in Toronto while Stan was on the road, but Stan was getting old, had pulled something in his arm on a trip overseas and needed help with the lifting.

"You think you're gonna see shit like that coming. You think something big enough to knock you right out of your life and into something new is going to make some noise on its way in. But it can happen like that. I tell myself it took two seconds to change my life, but that's just what the clock showed. When she changed her mind, whenever that was, it probably happened in no time at all."

They camped together once: Stan, his wife Louise, their friend James Cole and the woman James had been seeing for years, Janice Barber. They rented two canoes at an outfitter just inside Algonquin Park and set out across a wide, choppy lake for three days of tenting. Janice Barber always looked like she might go off and read a book at any moment. She paddled a canoe like the job might be washing dishes, like she intended to keep going until there weren't any more dishes in the sink. When spoken to, about almost anything, she said things like, "Is that so?", "I'm sure I didn't know that," and "Tell me more." In this way, she was the perfect companion for James Cole who was most content being listened to. Stan and Louise laughed quietly at the one-sided conversation in the other canoe while the four of them paddled slowly toward their campsite.

Jim's voice bounced off rock faces and came back at them from across the lake. Janice's short replies were lost in a breeze. None of them camped very often, and Stan could not remember why any of them had thought it might be a good idea for a vacation, the four of them, in one large tent, between a vast, dumb forest and a sullen lake. Midway through the second day, they found they would not have enough food for both dinner that evening and breakfast the next day. Stan set himself to canoeing back to the outfitter for cans of spaghetti. Just as he launched, Janice spoke her intention to join him. He sat, holding the canoe steady while she waded out and climbed aboard.

"Now don't go and get yourself lost on purpose," Jim shouted from shore.

"I'm sure I don't know what you mean," said Janice, too softly almost for Stan to hear.

They spoke in small clusters of words, not ever managing a full sentence on either leg of the trip. Janice said "a loon, there," and Stan replied "watch, chop." She wore a one-piece bathing suit cut squarish and low across the back. Stan watched her shoulder blades flex in and out with each stroke. As the paddle dug into the water, her suit would list away from the skin at her ribs and he would see the side of a breast, whiter than the rest of her.

"You know," Stan leans into Tony and drops his voice below the murmur of the party behind them, "even, what, over thirty years later I can remember the sight of that pretty young girl's breast, just the side of it, coming into view over and over again while she paddled. It's the kind of memory that makes a long train ride a bit more bearable."

"I'm sure I don't know what you mean," Tony said.

In the outfitter's shop, they worked opposite sections, Stan gathering the necessaries plus a few snack treats (potato chips, licorice, marshmallows for the fire), and Janice browsing the spinning rack of paperbacks, touching each spine as they glided by.

On the way back, they stayed close to the shore to avoid a building wind. It was less work in the shallows but made for a longer trip than the straight line across the lake they'd taken the day before.

In one small bay, Janice asked to stop and there she slipped over the side of the canoe and swam in clear amber water. Stan stayed seated and watched her. He laid his paddle across the rails behind him, leaned back and smelled the forest. Janice made no noise when her head slipped under or emerged from the water. She swam like an otter, smiling to herself about the pleasure of it.

They slipped back into their campsite around a jut of rocks and dwarfish trees.

"Fish, there," Janice said, and Stan looked on shore to see three small rock bass, red-eyed and lifeless beside a four-inch hunting blade jammed into the soil.

"James has been killing things again," she said.

Past the fish was an emptiness, immediately unsettling, like there wasn't still a tent just in the trees and gear all around; like it was just wind through underbrush. The yellow front flap of the tent breathed in and out, slowly and soundlessly. Stan watched the flap and, as they came ashore, he spotted a leg. Louise lay on her back, sleeping on the mattress of blankets and clothes spread across the tent floor. She snored lightly, and her hand lay limp across her chest. She was in her bikini. Her hair lay in wet ringlets on the pillow.

"I could do the same," said Janice, softly.

Using a log as a tabletop, Stan cut the heads off each fish, sliced them from tail to throat and removed the stomach sacks. He scaled them with the back of the blade and wrapped the meat in the largest leaves he could find. Then he buried the three little packages in the firepit, beneath the ashy, grey coals.

"There's still enough heat there," he said to no one. He covered the discarded scales, heads and tails with soil, thinking about bears.

Jim walked back into camp twenty minutes later. He walked directly to Janice and flung his arms at her waist in an attacking hug.

"I started out to get wood for the fire, but just kept going," he said. "There's people camping all around us, and it turns out we could have walked to this site if we wanted to. There's a path that cuts through about two hundred yards that-a-way."

His face and arms showed scratches from the brush, and his shirt was stained with sweat.

"I met some of our neighbours, but they didn't meet me—if you know what I mean."

"Everything's an espionage with James," Janice laughed. She screeched as Jim picked her up and carried her into the lake.

"And now, back to the underwater headquarters," he screamed, falling forward so both of them slapped into the water, all arms and legs and gasping.

"He's unstoppable, that man," Louise giggled.

Stan's young wife sat in the doorway of the tent, rubbing her fists against her temples, massaging herself awake. She looked at Stan and smiled tiredly.

That night, the four friends ate warmed spaghetti straight from the cans. Jim laughed loudly all evening, and made them all laugh many more times. The next morning they packed up and made their way back to the city.

"And I'll be damned if I didn't forget about those fish I put in the fire." Stan tapped the coaster in front of him with his empty glass, indicating to the young woman behind the bar the spot where his next beer should go. "Those three little fish were killed for no reason at all."

"What ever became of Janice Barber?" Tony asked. "You know, after the '51 series?"

"Well, I guess if I knew that I might not be sitting here with you, my boy."

"And wouldn't that be a shame?" Tony laughed.

"Wouldn't that be a goddamn shame."

Three

S tan did not get back to his house until after seven the next morning, almost nine hours after the two seconds that changed everything. Unsmiling, black-suited League officials had hidden him away in the Toronto general manager's office until well past midnight when all the newspapermen had finally given up and left the building to make their deadlines.

Among those in charge of running hockey, the incident remained unspoken of, something to be denied again and again, laughed off as ridiculous. Stan understood to keep his mouth shut while he was whisked away from the ice surface after the final whistle. A cluster of men hurried him through the inner corridors of the arena to the room furthest from inquiring eyes and ears. He knew better than anybody what had happened in the last few seconds of the game, and what it meant to the League. He knew all the details, and there wasn't one he wished to share with anyone.

A black hat was shoved onto his head and knocked down over his eyes for the trip past the photographers' bench. He was aware of several bright flashes and men calling out his name. He recognized the voices as those of reporters he'd said hello to in the hallways every other evening, but this evening he knew he was to pretend he didn't hear them. With the hat over his eyes, Stan saw only his own feet on the floor, tripping up several flights of stairs and crossing thresholds here and there until they were finally directed to a chair beside a large oak table in the GM's private meeting room. The door to the room banged shut against several more shouts and flashes and Stan was left in the relative quiet and darkness, two stern men in dark suits as his companions. Looking at the faces of the two men, Stan was aware he had lost his job, the greatest job he'd ever hoped to have. He made note of it in his head. The job was gone. When he closed his eyes, he saw his wife's face.

Nearing 1:00 a.m. the League president came into the office and dismissed Stan's two silent guards. He sat down across the table from Stan, took off his hat and laid it on the table in front of him. Stan could smell the sweat and Brylcreem coming from the older man's perfectly combed hair. The president had been talking to reporters and getting his picture taken since the end of the game. Stan heard exhaustion in his breathing.

"Stan," the president began with a sigh, and then veered off in another direction unwilling to get right to the point "… Stan, check that top drawer there in that desk. He's got to have a bottle of something in there."

Stan shuffled to the GM's desk, pulled a half-full bottle of bourbon from the drawer and sat back down.

"Well don't just look at it man, let's have a drink."

The bottle slid back and forth across the table several times.

"Stan," the president made another start, "I don't know what's going to happen next week or next month or next year. I don't know. But for tomorrow and the next day and certainly the next, someone else is the head timekeeper here in Toronto. We can't have you in the booth, Stan."

"My wife is sleeping with a man... another man, I mean." Stan hadn't exactly decided he wouldn't talk about what he'd seen during those lost two seconds, but he'd certainly never planned to be talking about it at that moment, just as he was being eased out of his job by a half-drunk sixty-year-old businessman in a sweaty suit. He said the words and then took a longer-than-average pull on the whiskey bottle.

"Well, Stan, I don't know what to say. That's a punch in the gut, isn't it?"

The president drummed his fingers on the tabletop and looked around the room uncomfortably. He had been expecting denials and apologies. These were things he was used to from his employees, and he knew how to muscle his way past them. But a confession like this; what was he supposed to do with this?

"Are you saying you did this on purpose, Stan?"

The bottle was empty when Stan spoke again. "It's the kind of idea you like to toy with in your head, isn't it? You like to think about what you'd do if you came home early one night and found... you know, like what happens in books. You like to think you'll have something to say about it."

"You're shook up, Stan. Did you understand what I said earlier, about tomorrow?"

"I understood."

"Where do you live, Stan? Let me give you a ride. I have a driver waiting downstairs." The older man looked at his

watch and started to mutter something about his wife waiting at home, but thought better of it. "You need to sleep this
whole thing off."

Stan directed the League driver to an address in Toronto's
far east end, where the streets finished themselves in wide
sand beaches. He had an idea what he'd find at home and
was in no hurry to get there. The car pulled up to the last
house on the street.

"You live here?" the president asked with undisguised suspicion, peering past Stan to the large front lawn and flower
borders of a lakefront mansion.

"We rent," Stan said as he climbed out of the car.

"You rent what? The garage?" But Stan had slapped the
black sedan's roof twice and the driver began inching away
from the curb.

"We're not done talking, Stan," the president shouted as
the car picked up speed. "I want you in my office in a week."

The beach was empty of people. Though the air was
warm for early spring, it was well past midnight and even
the boardwalk stragglers had wandered off home to bed.
Stan found the waterline and sat down in the wet sand. He
wanted to get calm and give the ringing in his ears a chance
to subside. He wanted to run through things in his head
and see if they still made sense, if the same conclusions
could be drawn. To his right was the glow of the downtown,
dominated by the steady red sign on top of the Royal York
Hotel. On his left sat the squat, brooding darkness of a water
filtration plant, unlit but clicking away in its gloom, preparing to help the city shower and get ready for another day.

The lake breathed a chilling mist in his face, and somewhere way out on the water a laker moaned in its engine,

invisible, bypassing the city for some more industrial port further west. For a long time he thought of nothing. He stared out into the misty water and just breathed. For a while he slept like that, sitting up, wrapped in his coat.

When he found himself awake and thinking again, he was running over a familiar memory. He remembered how his mother used to force him to finish his meals as a child. He recalled the nightly standoff before a plate empty of everything but broccoli or green beans or some other vegetable he'd decided to hate for a while. He laughed quietly when he remembered these struggles, since they were so futile and unnecessary. He didn't actually hate eating anything. He had an indifferent palate. Everything was just fine as long as it filled him, but there he was each evening, arms crossed, with his mother standing above him in a similar pose. A contest of patience. He wondered if she had enjoyed the game as well as he had.

He found himself standing, and then walking, his feet pulling him slowly toward home. There was no avoiding it. At some point, he would have to walk through the door and see that she had cleared out. At some point he'd have to admit to being alone. He might as well get on with it. He turned back toward land and crossed through a park to Queen Street. He turned west and walked the long quiet street leading downtown. At Woodbine, he stopped to wait out a light, though there were no cars on the road. He was beginning to feel tired. He was beginning to want his bed, no matter how empty, and suddenly he regretted the distance in front of him. The light turned green, but before he could move, he felt the strong grip of a man's hand on his arm, stopping him, pulling him backwards.

"Take it," the man said, his words full of spit and the stink of alcohol, "take it all, I don't want it any more."

The man had been slouched in a darkened doorway beside the intersection. Drunk and a little lost, he'd stopped in the doorway to relieve himself and had instead fallen asleep standing with his head against the bricks. Stan's impatient shuffle at the light had woken him. There was a brick pattern of lines in his forehead.

"I thought it was the perfect deal, you know," he said, crying a little as he used Stan for support, "but a man has to be a man. He just has to."

The drunk clung to Stan's coat, and Stan resisted the urge to push him off, certain they would both fall and not wanting to hear the sound of the man's head hitting the sidewalk. The drunk was clinging with his left hand, a strong left hand, and pawing at Stan with his right. At first, Stan thought he might be being robbed, the man seemed so intent on Stan's pocket, but then he realized the drunk was actually trying to give him money. The man's right hand was tensed to grip a large wad of bills and he struggled with Stan's coat, trying to get at the pocket so he could shove the cash inside.

"Say, what are you doing there, friend?" Stan said, wrestling the stronger man and knowing he'd surely lose. "I think you want to keep that for yourself. There looks to be an awful lot there."

The man seemed surprised to hear another voice in the night and he stood up straight. Stan used the opportunity to push him backwards against the wall.

"I don't need your money," he said. He couldn't think

of anything else to say. "I'm not a bum. I'm just going for a walk."

The drunk looked Stan up and down and laughed a loud drunken laugh.

"Did you have a little fight with the beach then?" he said.

Stan saw for the first time the effect of his half-sleep on the beach. The lower half of his black coat was soaking wet and covered in grey sand and pebbles. He wasn't a bum, but he sure looked like one.

"I fell asleep," Stan said, flicking tentatively at his coat with his fingers.

"Lucky you," the man said. "Got a cigarette?"

The two men stood at the corner of Queen and Woodbine, smoking. Stan kept his eyes on his companion, not relishing another dance with him, and wondered what would happen next.

"My wife is rich," the man said, adding smoke to his spit-filled conversation. "She's one of the richest women in the city. We live in a fucking mansion up there on the hill. Where the fuck am I?" He looked around to get his bearings. "Up that way."

"Sounds nice," Stan said.

"Sounds nice? Yes, it is nice. Nothing like being fucking rich, let me tell you. I did okay myself once. Boxing. I was a boxer—hard to tell, I know, what with my beautiful face and all, but I broke heads up and down the Great Lakes for ten years, and when I stopped boxing, I managed younger boxers. I made a fucking fortune."

"Sounds like you have it all figured out." Stan was enjoying his cigarette, enjoying the approach of morning, but getting more and more anxious for bed. He could feel exhaustion creeping up his legs from the cold side-walk.

"That's when I met her, my wife. She came to the fights one night on the arm of some other rich stiff, some art-loving prick who thought he knew something about everything. I saw them in the crowd and just hated the guy right away. I said to myself, I'm going to save that girl from herself. So, I went and took her way. We were married six weeks later."

"You're a man who knows what he wants," Stan said.

"She didn't need me or my money. Her father made millions in steel out of Hamilton. She didn't need anything I had to offer, but she wanted me, so we got married. Then those pricks fixed one of my boys and that was that. One prick little fighter takes one prick little fucking bribe and suddenly I'm giving all my money to lawyers."

"Mob?"

Stan had heard all the stories. The mob had even taken a run at hockey. The word was it didn't pan out for them, but who knew.

"Mob is right. Everyone was mob. The commission was mob, the prick fighter was mob, the fucking press was mob as far as I know. All I know is they emptied me. And she said she didn't care, she said that's not why she married me anyway. Now, every night she gives me a handful of cash and sends me out of the house so I won't get pissed up there and start breaking things. Now, I'm like a big dog she can't handle any more. I still get the good food, but I'm in the kennel sure as fucking anything."

"There are worse things," Stan says.

"What the fuck do you know about it?" The man tried to

raise his voice to a shout but lost heart halfway.

"I know about it," Stan said. "There are worse things than being pitied."

"Yeah, maybe, but not for me." The man rubbed his forehead under his hat, his huge right hand still wrapped around a folded brick of cash. "Look, are you going to take this or not? I don't have all night."

"Why would I take it?" Stan said.

"It's up to you," the man sniffed at him. "Either you take it, or the lake takes it. I know one thing, I'm not going to take it any more." The ex-boxer clamped his left hand on Stan's shoulder and, squinting, guided his right hand to Stan's coat pocket. The money slipped in like a smooth rock. He felt the weight of it immediately.

"Buy yourself something nice," the man said, tripping backwards a little as he released Stan.

"And if anyone asks you, you never saw me tonight. I don't want them dragging me out of the lake for her to look at. Just let me go. Maybe I'll wash up in New York some-where. Maybe I'll go over the Falls."

"The Falls go the other way," Stan said.

The man stopped walking backwards and looked Stan in the face. He started laughing. They both started laughing.

She typed the note. Stan knew this was her way of being polite, so he didn't have to look at her handwriting and become morbid about it. In books he'd read, the note had been the only thing left to remind the man of the woman, but this was not true for Stan. She'd left all her gardening utensils, including her prized stainless steel hand spade and the little mat she used to rest her knees on while weeding. Many of her books remained, the ones, he guessed, she never intended to read again. She had taken only one of her houseplants, the African violet. He'd suspected for years she had a special relationship with this plant and now he knew he'd been right. The ficus and the rubber tree stood where they'd always stood, though it looked like she'd dusted their leaves sometime in the last few days.

Otherwise, it had been a hasty leaving, he could tell, and with good reason. Recognizing what had happened, seeing that Stan had seen their hands laid casually one on the other, watching his face as he was dragged away from his timekeeper's booth into a mob of suits and reporters, Louise knew the time she'd been anticipating had arrived. She had Jim accompany her in a taxi to the house on Saulter Street; they'd thrown her essentials into a couple of suitcases, grabbed the African violet and left. The note told Stan that she'd taken the car—*they'd* taken the car—but he knew without having to be told. They wouldn't stay in the city. They would get away, far away, and for that they'd need a car.

Stan sat at the kitchen table. In front of him was his wife's typewritten, unsigned goodbye, and beside it on the tabletop, a neatly stacked pile of twenty-dollar bills. He'd counted them three times, to be sure of things. There was nineteen hundred dollars in the stack. What man needs almost two thousand dollars to have a good time for one evening? What kind of life must that be? Stan didn't worry that the drunk had jumped into the lake. He'd known drunks in his time. He'd listened to the remorse an evening full of whiskey can bring, and he knew it rarely prompted any serious action other than the kind of impulsive behaviour one generally lives to regret, like picking up a girl at the end of the night, finding yourself in an alleyway brawl, or giving away a pocketful of money because you feel sorry for how life's treated you. He felt sure the man was right now sleeping himself into a hangover on a chesterfield in his wife's luxurious mansion overlooking the lake. If he even noticed his missing allowance the next morning, he'd chalk it up to more bad luck and add it to his list of grievances against himself. Stan felt too sorry for himself to feel sorry for some poor drunk rich guy.

For the first time in years, Stan listened to a hockey game on the radio, at the local tavern up on Queen Street. He listened all the remaining games there, heard Toronto win the championship. When the final whistle blew, he pulled a small fistful of money from his jacket pocket and bought a round of drinks for everyone in the bar. He was grateful to the crowd in the bar. Stan's picture had been in the paper for a week following the game that had lost him a job and a wife, but if anyone did recognize him, they said nothing about his two-second mistake. They let him drink and enjoy their enjoyment of the games. For hours after the final game, Stan walked through the crowds on the street, watched them bang their pots and blow their horns.

In the early summer, Stan received a letter with a Winnipeg postmark. This note was handwritten (she'd left her typewriter behind). She apologized for the abruptness of her departure and for the way in which Stan had to discover her relationship with Jim. She was sorry he had lost his job and she hoped he'd be all right. She did not explain how it had all happened, the affair, the destruction of their marriage. She didn't have to. Since their wedding day, a hot day at City Hall, Stan had anticipated an ending much like this. He knew Louise was an ambitious woman, someone who longed to travel and see the world, someone who would not stay in one place for very long. He, on the other hand, would have been satisfied to spend the rest of his life as a timekeeper in Toronto, to see each year develop much the same as the last, with only the team's performance through the playoffs from year to year determining any difference. He often wondered what it was about him that convinced her to marry him in the first place.

He was, he knew, boring, and while he didn't mind being bored by himself, he couldn't imagine anyone else standing for it. If he'd been a stepping stone for her, he was a willing one. Temporary or not, Stan had loved his marriage and adored Louise. He couldn't bring himself to blame her for ending it. She had clearly given him more than he'd given her.

At the end of the letter, after wishing him well, Louise wrote that Stan could find his car at the corner of Main and Robert in Penetanguishene, Ontario. She was sorry to have taken it without asking, and sorry to not be able to return it, but she was certain it was safe and would remain where she'd left it until he could manage a trip up there to fetch it.

It was a five-hour bus ride to Penetang. Stan sat in a window seat beside an older woman who was going to visit her son in prison. Manslaughter, she said, over and over again. Stan told her he was visiting relatives. The bus left the station at Bay and Dundas in early orange light, picked its way through empty city streets and found countryside to the northwest. They sped past the tiny airport at Malton, a field and a windsock, and found the northern highway, number 27. Here the landscape was hills and trees, one farm bleeding into the next, and towns with curious names, each of them a brief stopping point for the bus—Kleinburg, Nobleton, Schomberg, Bond Head. Further north, near Barrie, Stan saw a sign for a town called Utopia.

The bus stopped for half an hour in Barrie to off-load some passengers and pick up others. Stan took the opportunity to stretch his legs. He walked along Dunlop Street past an artillery gun cemented to the sidewalk as a war memorial. Apparently, Barrie had sent more than fifty men to their deaths in two wars. So many for such a small town. Late morning light bounced off Lake Simcoe and shimmered between the shop windows on the street. Stan walked down to the water and gazed north, up the bay to where it widened and disappeared in distance. It looked so different from the lake he knew back in Toronto, so empty and wild. He imagined that people had stood in this spot for thousands of years and seen pretty much the same view. Trees and water and sunshine.

An hour and a half later, he was walking the streets of Penetang, looking out over a different bay on a different lake. He'd seen his car at the central intersection as the bus chugged past, and now he was trying to remember his way back to it. There wasn't much to the town, so he didn't worry about getting lost, but he had no other reason for being there, and an idea had begun to demand time in his mind. He wanted to get back to Barrie as quickly as possible.

The car was parked by the side of the road, across from

a furniture store. There was no ticket on the windshield, and no sign it had been tampered with in any way. Only in a prison town, Stan thought. It was unlocked and the keys were as Louise had described them, under the passenger side of the front seat. There was a full tank of gas. Stan imagined Louise insisting on it and Jim begrudgingly paying for the fuel. How does one get to Winnipeg from Penetanguishene without a car, Stan wondered.

The car had been sitting in the sun all morning, the air inside hot and stuffy. As he sat down on the driver's side, Stan was overcome by the smell of his wife's perfume. It was more than just the after-effect of her presence; it had been spilled into the upholstery somewhere on the back seat. He tried not to imagine how that had happened, and instead just opened all four windows before starting the car. He drove to the edge of town and found the highway south. In Barrie, he found Dunlop Street again and pulled to the curb beside the real estate office he'd walked past that morning. *Shoreline Lots*, the window said, *Prime Wooded Property*.

"Somebody's been having fun in this car," the sales-man laughed out loud and waved his hand in front of his nose. "Smells like Paris, if you know what I mean, and I think you do."

Stan was following the lakeshore roadway north out of town. Beside him sat Gino (Gene) Auden, sales agent for Simcoe Realty, specialist in vacation and cottage proper-ties.

"My folks were the first Italian family in Barrie, so they say," he boasted, shaking Stan's hand in the office. "Changed all our names right away to try and fit in, but I like Gino, it's more manly than Gene I think."

Gino Auden was a giant of a man, over six feet tall and easily more than 250 pounds. He kept his thinning hair shaved close to his head and sported a Clark Gable moustache on an otherwise perfectly groomed, perfectly round face. He had rings on four of his fingers, and his fingernails, Stan noticed, were perfectly manicured. He reminded Stan of many of the League higher-ups he'd met in his time. Men who took care of their appearance, who were certain of their power.

"I think you're going to like what I have to show you," Gino said, for the third time. "Cottage country is moving, you know. Muskoka's all well and good for those rich Toronto types, but ordinary schlubs like you and me deserve a place to relax as well, am I right?"

He is right, Stan thought. He'd never imagined even wanting to own land in the country, let alone being able to afford it, but that morning the pictures in the office window on Dunlop Street had enticed him, and the prices were suddenly within reach. Gino directed Stan along a single-lane country road crowded in by trees. The road ran along a ridge above Kempenfelt Bay. Here and there, the water shone blue through a gap in the forest. They drove through Shanty Bay, a hamlet of a dozen or so houses and one small whitewashed church, and eventually turned down toward the lake on a dirt road rutted here and there with washouts from a recent downpour.

"There's absolutely no development this far up yet," Gino said, pointing out the open window to the thickly wooded land crowding the shoreline. "Only the old-timers, folks who've lived up here year-round for a century or so. And you want them types around in case anything goes wrong.

It's awfully quiet up here at night, and dark. Nice to know someone's around even if they're a mile away, am I right?"

Again, there was no arguing with Gino. By his own count, his practised patter had sold fifteen lots along this stretch of Simcoe shoreline in the last five months.

"Right here will do, sir." Stan pulled the car to the edge of the road and stopped the engine.

"Are you ready for paradise?" Gino smiled at him from the passenger seat. He'd turned to face Stan and his body blocked the entire view from the passenger-side window.

The way down into the property from the road was a narrow cut through thick pines, untrimmed, their lower branches brushing the ground in wide skirts. Stan inhaled deeply the combined scents of evergreen and lake water. Squirrels leapt from tree to tree thirty feet above his head.

"That's *your* fresh air you're smelling, Stan." Gino slapped him on the back and took the opportunity of contact to pull him by the arm past the last of the pines, his left arm opening wide, like a maître d' showing off the prize table. What remained of the property was a deep grass meadow speckled with yellow dandelions and buttercups. Here and there, giant weeping willow trees bent their long soft branches to the earth around elephantine bodies. The land ended at large boulders falling away into the gently rolling waters of the lake.

"Christ Jesus," Gino sighed, looking out across the water, "if every showing looked like this I'd have none of these lots left. You've hit it on a great day, I'll say that."

The property was 150 feet wide and ran from road to lake another 150 feet, forming a near-perfect square. There was a small, falling-down cabin near the lake, doubling as living shack and boathouse, though no boat was present.

"The owner built that cabin in Shanty Bay and floated it here just as you see it. Easier than hauling the materials. That hazy patch of land there," Gino pointed directly across the lake, "is Georgina Island—Indian reservation, but don't worry, they can't get you all the way over here—and that close bit of land there just the other side of the bay is Big Bay Point. There's a lighthouse at the very end. Kind of comforting to look at after dark. If you head down the bay there you get back to Barrie and directly to the other end of the lake there is Orillia. You're about right in the middle. A prime spot if you ask me, but I'm just the salesman, what the hell do I know?"

Stan asked for a little time to himself, and walked back and forth across the shoreline, *his* shoreline he'd decided, while Gino smoked nervously back up by the car. Stan saw a family on this land. He saw continuance, and that was a lot better than anything he'd seen for himself back on Saulter Street. He could give himself no reason for the feeling; he was simply sure in his decision.

Back in the realty office on Dunlop Street, Stan signed all the papers and pulled the fifteen-hundred-dollar total from his jacket pocket.

"Hello, darling!" Gino yelled, drawing the attention of the two other salesmen in the room.

"Holy crap, man, if I'd known you were packing that much cash, I'd have hit you with a rock and dumped you in the lake."

"I know you would have," Stan said, and the two other salesmen laughed.

Four

The Cup went missing in the summer of 1952. It was gone for almost two months. No details of its disappearance or its whereabouts while it was gone have ever been publicly known. Stan Cooper, now the head custodian and cleaner at Maple Leaf Gardens in Toronto, found the Cup at centre ice one morning when he happened to be the first person in the building. Training camp for the new season had just begun, and the ice had to be maintained every day even if the team spent the whole day in the gym. He threw the switch for the secondary lights, and there it was. The League had never reported it missing. The police had never been consulted. A private investigator worked for three weeks but was eventually fired after falling down drunk in the League president's office while making a report. There were plans in the works to create a duplicate cup from photographs, and then one morning it just appeared at centre ice in Toronto.

Stan walked out across the centre line still carrying his coffee and doughnut in a paper bag. He had seen the Cup in this building many times. He had seen the Cup both won and lost in this building. He burned at the thought of seeing

the Cup being won. He felt a wave of nauseating embarrassment about it, and then embarrassment about being
embarrassed. He looked at his own face reflected in the perfect silver and thought about his wife.

He circled it, shuffling around the ice in his rubber-soled
work shoes, watching the shine and reflection in the dim
glow of the secondary lights. He reached out and pushed at
it to see if it would move. His hand left a dull smudge on the
silver. It was the only print he could see on the entire trophy.
Whoever had left the Cup there had polished it before they
left. Stan took a handkerchief from his pocket and wiped
away his fingerprints.

He put the doughnut shop bag on the ice beside the Cup
and jogged back across the rink to the timekeeper's booth
where he knew there was a phone. By the time he returned,
his coffee had melted a circle of water around the bag,
soaking the apple fritter inside. League officials arrived
within the hour.

While he waited for them Stan stayed on the ice, drinking cold coffee, one hand on the Cup. He helped carry the
trophy into a back office and watched as it was authen-
ticated. As they were putting it in the back of one of the
official League cars, one of the men turned to Stan and said,
"Well sir, I guess this makes up for that little fuck-up last
year," and then laughed, slapping Stan on the back with a
gloved hand.

Stan and the Cup were driven out of the city on the same
morning, bouncing down the Queen Elizabeth Highway in
the back seat of a black sedan. By noon they were in Wind-
sor, crossing the border, and at one that afternoon they were
both presented to the owner of the Detroit hockey team.

There were four other men in the room, one of whom Stan recognized as Sid Abel, Detroit's captain. Three months earlier, Abel had won the Cup, beating Montreal. He and his goalie Terry Sawchuk had been captured by a photographer hugging the Cup in the Detroit dressing room. The photo had been clipped from a Toronto paper and pinned in the lunchroom back in Toronto. Beneath it someone had written "In the arms of the enemy." Stan looked at the photo every day for weeks. He didn't agree with the inscription. Montreal was the enemy. By beating Montreal, Detroit had actually kept the Cup out of the arms of the enemy. When the Cup disappeared, so too did the photo and accompanying note.

Sid Abel shook Stan's hand hard. He smiled down at him and grabbed his shoulder with muscular fingers.

"You've brought my baby back to me, Stan."

"Yes sir," Stan said.

Sid turned to the men who had driven Stan to Detroit.

"Look here," he said, his tone turning angry, "everyone knows this is all Floyd's fault. If Floyd hadn't ended up face-first in the shitter when it was his turn to take the Cup, she never would have been nabbed. Floyd's an ass, we all know that. An ass and a goddamn drunk. And don't think we're ever letting him near this thing again, even if he scores the goddamn winning goal next year. But you boys gotta do something about this. Make sure it doesn't happen again. I mean, hockey players are going to get drunk at a party, you know what I mean? You can't just hand this thing over and hope it goddamn makes it back in one piece."

When Stan was loaded back into the sedan, alone now in the back seat, he had with him a brand new, handwritten contract from the League. He was to remain custodian in Toronto during the regular season and, in the summer, he would travel with the Cup, never letting it out of his sight. Sid Abel had put both hands on his shoulders and said, "The first goddamn thing he did was phone you guys—and he's from Toronto. I don't care what happened last year or whenever it was, Cooper here is your man."

Stan had felt like he was being pushed into the floor. His stomach turned liquid while they wrote out the contract, but he signed without hesitation. He was young enough and without his wife, summers were his own. Better to be on the road than alone in the house.

Back on the highway, one of the League men passed a leather-covered flask over the seatback.

"Shit Stan, you lucked out there. There's a dog-fuck of a job if I ever heard a one."

"What exactly do you do?" Stan asked.

"Fuck you," the man said, and both men in the front laughed loud and hard.

Stan felt himself laughing and was surprised. He hadn't laughed for real in over a year. He swallowed some gin and passed the flask back up front.

Five

A cool July evening in 1979, at the Hotel Royal in Göteborg, Sweden. Stan wheeled the Cup to his room using a luggage dolly he borrowed from the bell captain. The party had been short and respectful, one of the family- and officials-only events Stan preferred, since rarely did anyone get too drunk at one of these and make a mess he would have to clean. The formal ceremonies had finished early, around ten in the evening, after a nine-course meal and several rounds of toasts. The young champion Swede, Oleg Bandol, had moved his smaller party of friends from the dining hall into the hotel bar, giving Stan a chance to put the Cup to bed early for a change.

As was his habit, he closed the trophy into the bathroom, in the tub behind a drawn shower curtain, then locked and unlocked the room door several times to test for any quirks in the ancient mechanism. Leaving lights on and the room radio tuned to a jazz station, just loud enough to be heard from the hallway, he hung the paper *Do Not Disturb* flyer on the doorknob and slipped quietly down the stairwell to the ornate lobby. Having earlier sussed the entire hotel, Stan knew to turn left at the tiny bronze statue of a naked woman and continue through a small wallpapered door, out the staff entrance and into a short alleyway leading to Drottninggatan, a main street in the city centre. In this way, he need not cross in front of the threshold to the bar where the remainder of the party could be heard singing and laughing.

Rooms are made secure through ideas as much as through locks. Stan tried always to leave hotels by himself, while others believed him still there. He had a reputation among the players for always retiring to his room as early as possible and staying there until very near flight time. He ordered a schedule of meals ahead of time through room service to maintain a steady pattern of food trays on the floor outside his door. A careful eye would notice the plate covers had been untouched, but hotels are not places for careful eyes. Being the boring old man who slept with the Cup was a style he cultivated. It was his freedom.

Stan walked the darkened streets of Göteborg in a fog of cool salt air, following a long canal east out of the main tourist district and into the first ring of homes. In the car on the way from the airport, he had begun to orient himself with the grid, using the position of the sun to get a sense of the city's layout. Harbour to the southwest, municipal buildings in the east, houses in concentric rings from the centre to the suburbs. The front desks of hotels always had maps for the taking, and he would spend the short hours before any party, in any new city, studying the streets, delineating neighbourhoods and thumbing through the ads in local newspapers and telephone books for business addresses, marking out his route in his mind.

Such was his science that Stan rarely had any trouble

finding a good tavern or local restaurant in any city he visited. He had no interest in hotel bars and recommended tourist spots. His habit was to find the quiet rooms where people were comfortable, where they might even be bored, near where lives were lived and children slept. Since his divorce, a domestic life had to be borrowed, and Stan found most good-sized cities to be generous with these things, if you knew where to look. He preferred streets trimmed with sitting rooms where open windows spilled the sounds of conversation and favourite television shows onto the road. He liked to watch men talk with each other in low-voiced, finger-pointing intimacy.

Past the edge of the deep, black Trädgårdsföreningen Park, the stable squares of downtown began to soften and curve. He walked the broad avenue of Norra Gubberogatan, slowing to watch two young women buy cigarettes from a wall-mounted machine on the edge of a small traffic oval. He stopped behind them and fiddled with the foreign change in his pocket. It was scenes like this he watched for, evidence of the hidden life of a town. The girls smiled at him, took their cigarettes and continued on down the road. Stan watched them turn into a doorway less than a block away. He bought himself a soft package of Kents and walked the short distance to the tavern.

As often happened for Stan in new cities, the evening became a corner table, some sweet dark local beers and his cigarettes. The two girls from the street sat at the bar and talked each other into tears about something lost to him. Wives came to retrieve their husbands and stayed for a short drink themselves before heading home, all arms at elbows and comfortable laughter. Old men in hats played cards. There was a smell of fish and malted vinegar. A newspaper on the next table showed the handsome young Bandol, local hero, in front of the Cup at the airport reception the day before. Stan recognized his own shoulder in the corner of the shot. But for the crazy language and the extreme blondness and beauty of all the women, Sweden had the feel of Canada. If you ignored the age of buildings and looked instead at how people walked down streets, Göteborg might be Thunder Bay. Even in July, you could see boys carrying bundles of hockey sticks, giant gear bags slung over their shoulders.

When the tavern closed for the night, Stan walked the residential streets, observing the turning out of bedroom lights, the soft blue flickering of late-night televisions. An hour before the sun, he made his way to the harbour on the Skeppsbron. There, a small restaurant fed breakfast to fishermen and dockworkers. He ate a cold herring salad and drank more beer. Knowing, obviously, Stan was not a local, the cook tried out his English on him. He talked to Stan about relatives in Sudbury, about watching hockey at the Montreal Forum on a vacation ten years earlier. At sunrise, he poured a shot of vodka for himself and Stan, to toast the day.

Stan made his way back downtown through a morning rush hour of bicycles and fresh blond people walking the sidewalks with purposeful strides. Shops and offices opened, café owners cleaned tabletops in the early sunshine. He reached the hotel in time for the morning shift change. A new young man he'd never seen before was exchanging covered trays outside his room door, loading a still-full dinner tray onto his cart and placing a breakfast plate and coffee urn on the floor. Stan waited for him to wheel the cart down the hallway before trying his key. There was no sound of jazz from behind the door, and no light from underneath. The key stuck in the lock, at first refusing to turn, and he had to stand back and make sure of the number on the door.

He saw the Cup immediately as the shaft of light from the open door hit the bed where it stood, out of its case, gleaming like a child caught in a playful prohibition. Beside it, asleep on Stan's pillow, lay a young woman. She was curled on her side, one hand beneath her head, the sheet drawn to just below her shoulders, naked. She snored in a light, fluttering kind of way, and her blonde hair fell across her face. The Cup stood upright on the other side of the bed, bobbing slowly to the rhythm of her breathing.

Stan nudged his breakfast and coffee into the room with his shoe, and closed the door. He opened the curtains a crack and examined the Cup in a thin stream of morning light. Nothing had been added or altered and the bowl was empty. There were some fingerprints and hand smudges around the rim of the bowl and at the base, the only remnants of whoever had moved it from the bathtub. They were large fingerprints, male. Stan checked the bathroom next. A small overnight bag leaned in one corner of the counter, a toothbrush, lipstick and mascara beside it on the marble. The shower curtain was drawn just as he'd left it, and no towels had been used.

As quietly as possible, Stan removed his shoes and jacket, reclosed the curtain and stretched himself out on the small couch near the window. He listened to the beautiful snoring of the young woman and slipped into sleep. Less than an hour later he woke to the muted, almost imperceptible sound of bare feet on the carpet and turned his head in time to see a naked young woman glide into the bathroom. She returned wearing his bathrobe, picked up the breakfast tray from the floor and sat with it on her knees on the edge of the bed, smiling at him.

"You are Stanley," she said in perfect Scandinavian English.

"That's true," he responded, sitting upright and rubbing sleep from his eyes. His body ached for the bed and hours more sleep.

"You are not surprised to see me here?" the girl laughed.

Stan looked at her more closely. She could not have been more than twenty and, unlike almost everyone else in the city, she was not a real blonde. Her hair fell golden past her shoulders but it was streaked with dark that pooled at the roots. She let strands of it cover her eyes, and smiled coyly through them. She bit the insides of her mouth, which pushed her lips out in a nervous kissing motion.

"Not so surprised," he said, trying to return her smile. "The boys think this kind of thing is very funny."

The girl removed the stainless steel lid from Stan's breakfast and helped herself to a piece of bacon. She looked at the coffee longingly.

"Please, eat it all," he said. "I've had my breakfast. It would just go to waste."

"Yes, I am a joke," she said. "But you ruined the joke because you weren't here. Oleg told me to stay until you returned. He said you had probably just gone out for a walk. I listened to your music, I ate from your dinner tray, I watched a little television, but then it was so late."

Her name was Ana, and she was a prostitute, a student at the technical school who paid for her studies with dates. She was from across the water in Copenhagen where she had been raised the youngest of seven children, all boys but her. Her father worked at a brewery, brought his work home with him every night, and her mother had walked away from the house when Ana was nine years old, never to return. Ana assumed her mother was dead.

"Otherwise, how is it possible?" she said. "I have always thought she fell into a canal. It happens, people fall into canals and they are gone."

All this Stan learned in the first half-hour he spent with the beautiful young woman he had found sleeping in his bed. Ana had built her young professional reputation on a skill for massage and that irresistible nervous habit of biting the inside of her mouth. She worked all the downtown hotels and had a very regular clientele of visiting Danish businessmen and local politicians. Her specialty was something she called the knee massage. With the client face down on the bed, she would remove all her clothing, spread oil across the client's back, her own arms and knees, and climb aboard. She was small enough not to do any damage but just heavy enough to make a difference. She described the whole procedure to Stan, posing in the bed to show the posture.

"It is very soothing, and Oleg has already paid for it, so it is free to you. Come, take off your clothes. You look tired. I will put you to sleep in no time."

When Stan woke later that afternoon, he was again alone in his room. The Cup stood on the floor beside the bed where he himself had moved it. He felt rested and relaxed and his back was looser than it had felt in years. On the bedside table was a note written in green hotel pen ink.

Oleg wanted me to find out for him why you are called Two-Second Stanley. I will have to tell him I still do not know. Take care of yourself. Ana.

Stan first crossed the Atlantic Ocean with the Cup in order to escort it to Finland. This was in the 1970s, twenty years into his tenure as keeper of hockey's championship prize. In the almost twenty years that then followed his first trip, Stan crossed the Atlantic Ocean at least once a year, often more than once. His cabin home on Lake Simcoe contained hockey pucks and shot glasses from Sweden, Finland, Norway, Ireland, Iceland, Ukraine, Czechoslovakia and Russia. The Iceland trip was unplanned, an emergency refuelling stop on the way back from Norway. They were let off the plane to stretch and Stan had walked the trophy around the outpost tarmac, amazed at the rawness of the landscape. Jagged rock peaks surrounded the airport and steam rose from fissures in the land all around. He told himself he'd make a special trip back there someday, but never did.

Twice in his travels, Stan was detained at borders under the suspicion the Cup or its case was being used to smuggle something in or out of the country. In 1985, the Cup was confiscated at the airport in Prague. Stan stayed awake for thirty-six hours in an airport detention cell waiting to have the Cup returned to him, and then refused to board a plane until he himself was allowed to dismantle the trophy in the airport and make sure nothing had been altered or removed. Ten armed guards watched and laughed at the old man from Canada unscrewing the bowl from the top of the trophy and sticking his arm into it up to the shoulder, feeling around inside for whatever might have been left there in the time he had lost touch with it. When he pulled out a Czech flag, the room erupted into laughter and cheers.

Flashcubes bounced off polished silver. Smiling and shaking his head, Stan respectfully folded the flag and handed it to the nearest guard, but the armed man insisted he take it with him. Then in turn, as though somehow these men had not had enough of it in the preceding thirty-six hours, each guard ran his hand along the side of the Cup.

Over the years, Stan had removed hundreds of stickers and decals from the sides and especially the bottom of the Cup. He had untied countless neckties and pairs of suspenders attached beneath the bowl, fished out any number of folded notes and foreign bills slipped behind the nameplates, and unscrewed at least three false plates containing the names of local dignitaries, children and historical figures, one, in fact, bearing the name of the Pope. From the bowl, at the end of parties, Stan had removed pieces of cake, an entire roasted turkey, numerous cigars (some uncut and still in their wrappers), many sleeping cats, and exactly twenty-three pairs of panties, sixteen bras and three garter belts. Once, in Stockholm, he woke to discover the entire Cup, top to bottom, had been painted yellow.

Late in life, Stan calculated he had cleaned or polished the trophy approximately 4,560 times, an average of at least once a day, every day, four months of every year for thirty-eight years.

Since the day in ⁷2 he touched the Cup at centre ice in Toronto, he ha   ed it again an uncountable number of times. In the history of the Cup, no other person has held, lifted or touched it more than Stan Cooper. He lifted it on and off airplanes, trains and ships. He rode with it in the back of an ox-drawn cart, the front of an ocean-going canoe, a hot-air balloon and four different cable cars.

In late August of 1991, the Cup was returning to Canada on a transatlantic flight from Moscow. Stan had spent a week in Russia, escorting the trophy to the celebrations of two different players. It had been an uneventful trip as foreign visits go. There was the usual unending supply of vodka to be poured from the bowl, but this time, thankfully, no one had vomited into it. At one party, Stan noticed two very well-dressed men about whom people whispered and pointed from the edges of the room.

There was something in the perfection of these men and in their easy disregard for everyone else, something that smelled of violence. Other people's reactions to these men made Stan nervous for the Cup. But they seemed bored by the trophy; they ignored it and instead wandered the room in slow circles, boldly appraising the local girls with their eyes. The young Russian hockey player pulled Stan aside.

"Two-Second, don't worry," he said morosely. "They are here for my money, not your cup. They do their business as quietly as possible. Taking your cup would make too much noise. They don't want to be noticed; they just want to be paid."

Stan relaxed, and found himself experiencing an unexpected and unfamiliar pity for the young athlete. The older Stan got in his job, the less he had in common with the players who won the Cup. Though he'd never much participated in the shit slinging and underwear grabbing that seemed to entertain Cup-winners when he was a young man, at least they had shared a history as adults. With the kids he chaperoned later in his career, there was rarely anything of substance to be said, and he often could not even communicate with them. Their English vocabulary was held within the confines of the rink. Over the years as well, these young men became richer and richer, pushing an even greater divide between them and the older underpaid man who carried their trophy for them. What do you say to a boy in his early twenties who owns his own helicopter? How do you make small talk with the kid who buys prostitutes by the half-dozen?

But the Russians were often different. They liked their fun as much as anyone, but, as in the case of this young man, they had troubles their Canadian teammates could not guess at or imagine. With their giant paycheques came immense notoriety back home, and with the notoriety, trouble. In a country where a meal at the new Pizza Hut could cost a month's wage, the salary of a hockey star was an obscene temptation. These players paid out hundreds of thousands of dollars in protection for the privilege of returning home to an intact family. They themselves were never threatened. The local mobs would never cripple their winning horse. But the weight of generations of relatives hung around their necks. The flights to Moscow with the Cup were never quite as raucous as the flights to Moose Jaw or to Thunder Bay. And at this particular party, celebration of the Cup came second to celebration of the payoff.

Each new Cup-winning player in turn learned Stan's hated nickname and used it endlessly despite objections. He was convinced half the kids didn't even know why he was called "Two-Second" Stan, but they all liked the name, and liked even more that he so obviously hated it. With the foreign players, for some reason, it was often easier to remember "Two-Second" than his actual name, a convenience that meant, in other countries, he was introduced as a slim measurement of time.

In 1991, Valeri Berschin was one of the earliest young Russians to enjoy the curse of winning the Cup. On the ice, he was a goal-scoring surgeon, cutting past defenders with a combination of raw speed and brilliant fakery. Stan had been present for his game-winning goal in game five, a subtle backhand chip into the upper corner. The boy had not even been looking at the net, or the puck. In fact, he'd been looking at nothing at all. The slow-motion replays clearly showed a smiling Berschin with his eyes closed, scoring by instinct and feel. As the puck left the tip of his stick blade, he took the inevitable hit in front of the net, spun deftly on the toe of one skate and did not open his eyes until his back hit the end boards, his arms wide to receive an avalanche of teammates.

It was, in terms of raw skill and artistry, the greatest goal Stan had ever witnessed. And now the same young man stood by a table weighed down with food and drinks, sheepish in an uncomfortable-looking brown suit, the servant of two huge men with bad reputations. Stan waited until the evening wore on a bit louder and drunker, then approached Berschin.

"Look at the Cup, my boy," he said.

The young man blinked and downed the last third of a tumbler of vodka. "Two-Second," he said, smiling and drunk. "Yes, the Cup. What about it?"

"Do you own the Cup?" Stan asked.

"No, Two-Second, you own the Cup. I know. I can win it, but only you can own it. You've told me this before."

"Do those two mobsters own the Cup?" Stan asked.

"Two-Second, no, I told you already. You own the Cup."

"So, look at the Cup. You will take all that money you're making because you won this Cup, and you'll divide it up and it will all go away into the world. All that money is long gone already, some to your family, some to these two guys, some to you. Do you think this Cup gives a shit about your money?"

"I guess, no, I don't know what you mean." He was blinking now, trying to see Stan's point through a clear vodka fog.

"Stop thinking about these two guys. That's just life. Everyone's got his shit to deal with. They're your shit, so deal with them, but don't let them ruin this, this moment when this Cup, which you do not own and never will no matter how many fancy goals you score, this Cup is here for you. It's a short time, believe me. Tomorrow, I take this Cup away from you, we're back on a plane and you, my boy, you may never touch this Cup again after that. Stranger things have happened. Have you ever heard of Bill Barilko? Compared to that fact, those two big uglies mean nothing. You get my point? I see you standing around worrying about two men who will steal your money. You want to worry about someone in this room, worry about me, because it's me who will take this Cup away tomorrow."

"Two-Second, you win. You are the scariest man here." The young man smiled and slapped Stan between the shoulder blades. "From now on, I worry only about you."

"Some day, Berschin, trust me, you'll be closing your eyes and chipping rocks through your fence rails out there, rather than chipping pucks past goalies in the finals. When hockey is through with you it will let you know, believe me, and then those gangsters will be through with you as well. There's always another fucking superstar."

Berschin nodded and refilled his glass from one of the dozen clear, half-empty bottles on the table in front of him. "You are the wise old man of the Cup, yes Two-Second?"

"Damn right," said Stan, and walked away, trembling from sudden anger. It was a cruel speech in many ways, and a kindness. It made him feel briefly equal to the brilliant young player, an unfamiliar but satisfying feeling. On his way past the bar, Stan made a point of introducing himself to the two gangsters. Not caring if they understood him, he shook hands with them and looked each of them straight in the eyes.

The next evening, on the flight from Moscow, Stan fell asleep immediately after dinner. He'd felt all day as though a cold were coming on, and was glad this would be his last trip overseas for the season. The Cup sat secured in its case and strapped in with a seat belt in the first class seat beside him. He always gave the Cup the window seat, as that kept him between it and the curious who walked by it over and over on every flight.

Sometime between dinner and their initial landing in Montreal, over the Atlantic, Stan Cooper's heart stopped beating. The cold and indigestion he had been feeling was, in fact, a building infarction, and Stan passed on as he'd always hoped to, in his sleep with the Cup beside him. Because he died unnoticed while crossing time zones, no accurate time of death would ever be assigned to Stan.

The death of "Two-Second" Stan, of pulmonary infarction at the age of 72, was a problem for the airline flying his body home. The flight did not end until Toronto, but Stan's death was discovered on the descent into Montreal, by a startled cabin attendant trying to wake him. Normally, the body of a passenger who died inflight would be removed from the seating area at the first opportunity. Bodies were then transferred into thick cardboard carrying cases, and stored with the luggage below decks.

While there was enough room in storage for both Stan and the trophy, the airline worried about its legal and financial liability around the Cup. The trophy had boarded the plane as a passenger and was considered the property and responsibility of Stan Cooper, its keeper. This was the standard agreement the League made with airlines in order to ensure Stan kept his eyes on the trophy at all times.

With Stan out of the picture, and no other League representative on the flight, the airline lawyers worried that liability would transfer to them, and they didn't want it, not even for the short forty-five-minute hop from Montreal to Toronto. No one they contacted could put a price on the historic trophy.

Stan and his beloved Cup were both carried from the airplane at Dorval Airport and stored under armed guard, in an empty hospitality suite owned by the airline. In an obituary in the Montreal *Gazette*, one writer suggested this wrinkle was Stan's way of finally delivering to Montreal the Cup that was rightfully theirs, the Cup he'd stolen away with his famous two-second blunder in 1951.

The League sent Antonio Chiello to make the pickup. Tony worked with Stan at the head office in Toronto, and had helped him prepare the Cup for travel for the last two years. Tony rode to Montreal, a passenger in the hearse the League hired to care for Stan's remains. Childless and divorced, Stan had been the last of his line of Coopers for over twenty-five years. Tony Chiello was the closest he'd had to family.

Six

Only once, in August 1989, had Stan run across a situation with the Cup he felt he couldn't handle on his own. The championship trophy had been booked for a party by a young left-winger named Dalton Gunn, in his hometown of Eganville, Ontario, a five-hour drive from Toronto. It was a standard weekend job—drive up on the Friday night and figure out the town, shepherd the Cup all the next day when an impromptu tour of the townsfolk would be begged of him, stand watch during the drunken Saturday night festivities trying not to get too in the bag himself, and sneak the trophy back out of town before sunrise and the mischievous hangovers of Sunday. He'd pulled this job countless times in countless small towns within a clear day's drive of Toronto.

Stan packed the Cup in a League van, and took the northern route. He left Toronto at its top end, on the two-lane Highway 7, avoiding for the most part the bung of weekend cottage traffic that plagued the major highway routes. It was a slow drive all the same and, just before sunset, Stan pulled into a provincial park to eat the sandwiches and cookies he'd packed for himself. He parked the van as close to water as he could get, rolled down all the windows and ate looking out across a short expanse of lake to a massive stone bluff. The park brochure told him the cliff was home to First Nations petroglyphs carved high above the water, but he couldn't see any such things from his seat. The cliff face caught the last light of day, and Stan sat on after his food, enjoying the reflected heat radiating down on him.

Eganville was two more hours to the north, and Stan kept a careful watch at the road edges for deer. Early evening was a restless time for deer, he knew, and more than once on his many summer drives Stan had been forced from the pavement by a wandering doe. Once, in thick fog, he had just missed a large buck that had lost its footing on the slick pavement and crashed to his haunches trying to escape Stan's headlights. The desperate animal bucked and twisted in the middle of Stan's lane and he had to watch carefully while he steered past, to make sure the poor thing didn't bang a hoof or antler against his fender in terror. For the rest of the fog, Stan slowed the van below sixty kilometres an hour, and honked his horn at regular intervals. If he hit a mature buck at high speed, chances were they'd both be killed by the impact, and then who knows what would happen to the Cup, abandoned in favour of death on a deserted northern roadway.

Stan reached Eganville by ten o'clock, and checked into the hotel on the main street. Above a certain latitude, the Canadian towns Stan visited for his job pretty much followed the same plan. A central main street near either a river, lake or rail line, a compact collection of local businesses and services huddled together in a clump around the central intersection, a small school, usually at least one church (sometimes as many as three even for the smallest populations), a hockey arena, some kind of local diner, a gas station, and a hotel with a tavern on the main floor. Eganville followed the plan.

Stan secured the Cup in his room, tested the door lock several times and descended to the tavern by a creaking back staircase that smelled alarmingly of woodsmoke and grease.

"That better be the kitchen," he mumbled. "I sure as hell don't want to be jumping out a window in the middle of the night with that frickin' Cup on my back."

For a Friday night, the barroom was surprisingly empty. He hadn't seen another bar of any kind on his quick circle around the town, which could only mean that this place was such a shithole not even those without options bothered with it. Yet this was the room scheduled for the Cup party the next night. Stan acquainted himself with all the exits, including the locked and barred emergency door at the end of the dark hallway to the washrooms. He expected a rough crowd. Dalton Gunn wasn't much of a talent as a hockey player. His skill was hitting opponents in the face with his fists so hard they had to leave the game for stitches. A boy doesn't just get that way on his own. In Stan's experience, enforcers were not born, they were made by their upbringings—made by their towns. Stan checked out the small plywood podium built near one end of the pool table, obviously meant to hold the Cup and maybe a speaker. It was a clear four strides from that makeshift stage to the base of the back staircase, an easy escape from just about any trouble in the main barroom. The hotel owner had followed Stan's written instructions. He relaxed, and

wandered back to a bar stool where he intended to spend
the rest of his evening.

Including Stan, there were exactly six people in the room.
A group of three older men, longtime townsfolk by the
looks of them, light plaid jackets and baseball caps sporting farm machinery logos, sat around a small table near the
front door, watching the late news on the television above
the bar. A woman in her early thirties worked the bar, and
what looked to be either her boss or her husband sat at the
bar's far end, counting five-dollar bills into piles beside his
drink. The old men smoked without a break, lighting new
cigarettes from the last heat of their dying ones, and hardly
said a word to each other. In fact, everyone was smoking,
and Stan joined the party, pulling a pack of Export 'A' from
the breast pocket of his shirt. They had all watched Stan
checking out the bar, knew for certain he wasn't from the
town and figured out who he was right away. Stan caught
the words "from the League" mumbled across the far table
once or twice, but whenever he looked over at the old men,
their heads were turned to the TV.

"You just want a drink, or you looking for the show?" The
woman smiled tiredly at Stan, and placed a napkin in front
of him on the bar.

"What's the show?"

The far table broke into a low rumble of laughter. "Get
the show," he heard mumbled from beneath a ball cap.

"You're looking at the show," the bartender said, glancing
in a meaningful way down the length of her body. "It's five
bucks for the show. One song on the jukebox. I can go on
the pool table or just standing there in front of you."

"I'll take an Export," Stan said, "for now."

The woman smiled again, turned and snatched a beer bottle from the fridge behind her.

"A double Ex man, eh? You'll get the show," she laughed. "I know people, and you're the kind of guy who gets the show. Two more of those ought to do it."

"You're probably right," Stan laughed.

At midnight the man at the end of the bar walked to the front door and locked it. He returned to the bar and everyone in the room kept drinking. An hour later there was banging at the door and the man walked over again, checked through the curtains and slipped the lock, locking it again behind a group of four young men, also all in plaid jackets and baseball caps.

"Shift's over," Stan heard from the old man's table.

The young men ordered a table full of draft beer, delivered in small glasses by the trayful, in three runs. They called out for the show, and piled five-dollar bills on the edge of the pool table. In between songs the bar girl wandered the room in her G-string, making sure everyone had drinks. Her body showed signs of children, and was impossible to ignore. She stood beside Stan for a few minutes smoking a joint and laughing at the young men who howled from beside the pool table.

"Cooooome ooooon, Shelly. Put on that fucking Johnny Cash and get to it. I gotta get up early and work a whole damn shift before the party."

"Hold this," the woman said, handing Stan her half-finished joint. "These dicks will tear the fucking room apart if I don't shake it some more. You all right, honey? You got enough to drink?"

"I'm just fine."

Stan held the joint until it burned down too close to his skin, then he dropped it on the bar top. The man at the end of the bar walked over and scooped it up into the palm of his hand, ignoring that it was still lit. He popped it into his mouth and sat back down. The young men piled more five-dollar bills on the edge of the pool table. The three old men watched a black and white movie on the TV.

When Tony arrived the next evening, the victory party had been going for almost twelve hours. Pickup trucks lined the main street on both sides, clustered closer together near the hotel. The street was made impassable by partygoers a block in each direction from the front doors of the tavern. The town had been shut down, and the local police looked to have joined the celebration. Tony left his rental car on the nearest side street and pushed his way through the crowd into the hotel. The room was hot and smelled of sweat, beer and smoke. It was hard work pushing against the party, clearing a path for himself through bodies to the bar. He caught sight of Stan while still a good ten feet away. The older man was waving at him from the bar top, standing above the crowd.

"Some asshole." Stan waved Tony's attention past him to the wall behind the bar.

"Some asshole with a hate on for Gunn."

Between two framed mirrors, surrounded by glass bar shelves full of liquor bottles, the unmistakable scalloped silver bowl of the trophy protruded from the back wall of the tavern. Tony stared hard, but couldn't quite figure out what he was seeing.

"Where the hell's the rest of it?" he yelled to Stan, still inching his way through the crush.

"That's it—that's the whole damn thing. Some asshole with a hate on for Gunn took the thing and shoved it into the vent. The fucking Cup is stuck all the way into the wall for Christ's sake. I tried every goddamn thing I could think of before I called the office. I've been standing here just watching over it the entire time you been coming here."

Tony reached the bar, and Stan reached a hand down to help him up onto the countertop. The two men surveyed the situation, Tony leaning right across the gap and bracing himself against the back wall. Two waitresses criss-crossed beneath him, grabbing beer bottles and flinging their caps off without worrying where they might land. With one hand, he grabbed the edge of the bowl and applied pressure, pulling it toward him. There was no give. The trophy had been wedged into a space not quite big enough to hold it. Tony pushed off from the wall and swung back to stand beside Stan.

"This?" he yelled, motioning at the ridiculous scene. "This is why you told me to bring my tools?"

"We've got no choice," Stan said. His face looked crumpled with worry. "These people don't give a shit. Look at them. A couple of them tried to help me at first, but I had to stop them 'cause they're all fucking drunk and I thought they were going to crack the thing apart trying to wrench it out of there."

"Okay," Tony said. "So, what am I supposed to do if a bunch of guys bigger than me couldn't get it out of there?"

"We're opening the wall—no way around it. The League's just going to have to cover the damage."

"The League? What about the dick who rammed it in there?"

Stan waved his hand at the room.

"Right. Go get his name. He was wearing a plaid jacket and a baseball cap with some farm logo on it."

Tony looked out over the crowd, a sweaty, smoking mob of plaid coats and green caps. A young guy stood near the bar smiling up at him, like he was watching his favourite show. He winked when Tony's eyes crossed his.

"Fine. We're opening the wall. When?"

"Right now. Let's get the fucking thing out, and get out of this town."

"You want me to tear a wall apart in the middle of a party."

"Like they'd notice. Just get your goddamn tools. I'll help where I can, but I'm too fucking old to swing a sledge."

It took the two men less than an hour to open a two-foot square hole beside the vent, digging back into the wood frame construction of the old building. The waitresses and bartender worked around them the entire time, after removing all the glass and bottles from the wall. Every swing of the hammer Tony took was followed by loud cheers from the crowd, and the jukebox played nonstop.

Balanced on a ladder that Stan held, Tony crawled into the hole to his waist and cut away the side of the vent with a pair of heavy snips, taking care not to nick the side of the trophy. He chewed on a small steel flashlight and breathed dust. When he pulled back the vent it sliced into his finger, but he just kept working, not wanting to pull out and then have to crawl right back into that godawful spot. When the light hit the trophy, Tony read the name *Maurice Richard*. He slid his hand down the silver and felt past the pedestal bottom. Getting leverage, he gave a gentle pull, and the whole trophy moved to his pressure.

"It's loose," he shouted, and felt Stan's hands on his belt, pulling him back and supporting him while he gained his balance on the top of the ladder. Slowly, with Stan and the bartender below him bracing the trophy sides so it wouldn't scrape against the sharp edges of the dismantled vent, Tony pulled at the bowl of the Cup from a position on the bar. They worked the trophy through the smoky air and placed it gently on the bar. The tavern exploded in cheering and the spraying of beer. One of the waitresses tossed Tony a bottle of beer and he drank long, washing down dust. He smiled down at Stan and made like he meant to pour some beer into the Cup in celebration.

It was only then that he noticed a long dark red streak of blood, his own blood, running the length of the trophy, from the edge of the scalloped bowl to the pedestal. He looked down at his hand, from which more blood dripped steadily onto his shoe. He felt suddenly weak, and crouched onto a knee. Stan helped him off the bar, and wrapped his hand in a bar towel soaked in old beer.

When Tony had his strength back, he and Stan each took a side of the trophy and worked their way through the front door and the crush of people in the street to the back lot of the tavern where Stan's van was stashed. Tony watched over the Cup while Stan got the tool box, trophy case and his overnight stuff. They secured the trophy in its case and Stan climbed into the driver's seat.

"What are you doing?" Tony asked, still stunned from exhaustion and blood loss.

"I'm not keeping this thing here another goddamn night.

No telling what they'll do to it next. I'll give you a couple minutes to get to your car, but then I'm cutting out of here."

"What about the wall?"

"Fuck the wall. I'm never gonna see the inside of that room again. I'm getting out of this town and if anyone gets in my way I'm knocking them down."

Tony drove behind Stan down the black highway, his hand throbbing. At the juncture with Highway 7, Stan pulled the van into an all-night truck stop. They loaded up on coffee, and Stan stood a long time beside the van, smoking cigarette after cigarette.

"Can they do anything about the scratches?"

"They'll do something. They got silversmiths."

"You see that guy following us? He was on us for a hundred clicks before he turned around."

"Must've run out of beer."

"This kind of thing happen to you often?"

Stan sighed and coughed. He lit another smoke. "It's too bad," he said. "I think tonight I was going to get more than just the show."

Seven

Tony arranged for Stan's body to lie overnight at a funeral home on Ontario Street in downtown Montreal. He'd brought a casket with him from Toronto, and didn't want everything left at the airport any longer than it had to be. The driver of the hearse, Fred, a thin man in a shiny black suit that looked two owners removed from the thrift shop, helped him place Stan in the casket and the two of them loaded it and the Cup into the back of the hearse. Fred took no special notice of the Cup, as though he had no idea what it meant. Tony booked lodging at the Sheraton downtown, one room for himself and the Cup, another for Fred.

Tony and Fred had come to know a great deal about each other on their afternoon drive to Montreal. In his early twenties, Fred played saxophone in a jazz combo and worked at the funeral home for steady money. He talked about Montreal the entire trip, about jazz clubs, gangsters and beautiful women. Fred had played a few gigs in the city the year before, and fallen in love with a woman who worked the bar in one of the clubs. Since they ended, he hadn't been back, but he was ready to try his luck again. It was Tony's first visit to Montreal. He'd worked for the League for five years, but had been steady at the office in Toronto.

"Well, if you're interested in jazz, stick with me tonight," Fred advised. "I know at least five places within three blocks of each other. They'll all take your head off. Too bad they didn't send us here next week 'cause then there'd be the festival and you wouldn't be able to turn a corner without hearing jazz. If it's women you're looking for, just walk into any bar and open your eyes. There's strip clubs like crazy on Sainte-Catherine's, but they're all pros, you know. It's simple and hassle free, but not very warm, you know what I mean? You want to meet someone, Saint-Laurent is where the French girls hang out—and trust me, when you're in Montreal, you want to meet a French girl. Break my fucking heart."

"I'm not leaving the hotel tonight, Fred," Tony replied. "I've got to watch the Cup."

"What's the Cup going to do?"

"Without me, I don't know, that's the problem. It's my job to watch that Cup."

"That's some important cup then?"

Tony turned in his seat and looked at Fred. He'd already mentioned the Cup several times on the 401. They had carried it together in its black case from the security lock-up at Dorval and slid it in beside Stan's casket. Now they were driving with it into downtown Montreal, the city that had won the Cup more than any other city, the city that by rights owned the Cup. If they were to stop on the side of the freeway and pull the Cup out of its case, they would cause a huge traffic jam with people pulling over to get a look at it. If the citizens of this city knew that tomorrow Tony would be taking the Cup out of Montreal and driving it to Toronto, they would blockade Highway 401.

The Cup meant more to more people in Montreal than any jazz club or beautiful bartender ever would, and yet here was a young man, of hockey-playing, hockey-watching age who had seemingly never even heard of it. It was absurd. Tony had played with a miniature replica of the Cup in his crib. He had won and lost that little plastic Cup over and over playing table hockey with his friends. Each year he had begun the playoffs with the plastic Cup in his hand, waiting for Toronto to win so he and his father could drink champagne from it like he'd been promised. And each year, he didn't drink champagne from it. He had seen the real Cup at the Hall of Fame when he was ten, and again every year since then until the League hired him. Since that day, he knew exactly how many times, the actual number of times he had been allowed to touch the Cup. Helping Stan with his travel schedule, and getting him ready for almost every trip for the past three years, Tony had been asked to pick up the Cup seventy-four times.

Tonight had been seventy-five, and number one for Fred, though Fred wasn't aware anything significant had occurred. Tony looked at Fred and wondered what it must be like to be unaware of this cup.

"Yes, it is an important cup. Valuable anyway."

"Valuable? A trophy? How much could a trophy cost?"

"Well, Fred, think of it this way. You think we've been sent here to pick up poor old Stan, the guy in the back there, but if it weren't for that cup beside him, old Stan would have ridden home in the belly of an airplane beside people's pets and luggage. That cup is the only reason Stan is getting this great chauffeured ride back to Toronto. So, once something like this cup is more important than a person's dignity, how much would you say that thing is worth?"

"That's one fucking important cup, then."

In his hotel room on the twenty-third floor of the Sheraton, Tony removed the Cup from its case and set it on the floor near the window. He liked jazz and he liked women. Before leaving for the evening, Fred had stopped by Tony's room and marked out some likely hotspots on a tourist map.

From his window, looking north toward the mountain, the city lay itself before him in a blanket of shimmering lights. A warm breeze came through the screen and with it, the sound of female laughter from the street below. Tony lay down on the bed and let his hand brush against the polished chrome nameplates. He read the name Lanny MacDonald. He ran his thumb along the word Calgary. He listened to the city that truly owned the Cup, and fell asleep touching it. Seventy-seven.

Tony had all the right scars in all the right places to be a professional hockey player. At seven, playing pickup at Riverdale Park he took a puck off his right cheekbone and crumpled to the ice in a classic pose, blood pouring from his face, pooling black-red beneath him. The emergency room doctor put thirteen stitches into him, joked about his black eye and told him to rub vitamin E oil into the wound once it closed, to decrease the scarring. His mother showed him how to squeeze the oil from vitamin capsules, and once the wound closed Tony diligently flushed one capsule each night, making sure none of the oil came anywhere near his scar.

Three years later at an opponent's elbow, he lost a tooth he had only just grown and had to be fitted for a tiny upper plate. A white ravine ran through the black hairs of his left eyebrow, the result of a high stick at shinny. Another scar, on his upper lip, from too forceful a punch with a frozen glove when he was twelve, meant later in life he would never be able to wear a moustache as the whiskers would not fill in properly over the dead white tissue.

Tony played hockey in every season, as a kid rising rapidly through the levels of the organized sport in winter and captaining his own teams on the concrete rinks of summer. He surprised coach after coach by volunteering immediately to play defence. Every year Tony stood alone at the sideboards, the only defender until other failed forwards were assigned to join him. No one except Tony volunteered to play defence. As in all sports, the stars of the game are the front men, the goal-scorers, but Tony viewed defencemen as specialists, players who made it their business to be better than the front men, to stop the goal-scorers.

If not more glamorous, then certainly more noble, Tony's Cup-winning dreams were low-scoring. He was the guy who lay down in front of a slapshot and took the puck in the ribs for the team. The guy who muscled superstars away from the net and absorbed all their anger and ambition. Protector of the goalie, owner of the blue line, Tony wanted every game to end 1-0 for his team, in overtime. For any other young player with Tony's level of skill, choosing defence would have been a brilliant strategy for advancement. A young, talented kid who had already adopted the mature, team-playing mentality of a defensive specialist. A kid who didn't need to have his goal-scorer ambitions beaten out of him by coaches, teammates and opponents unconvinced of what was being offered, this was someone welcome at the upper levels of the game. As Tony would have been, but for his size.

"You should have gone into wrestling," was the parting consolation offered Tony when he was cut from his final team. All his skills and scars in place, Tony had simply not grown the extra four or five inches necessary to stay standing as a defensive specialist staring down forwards his own age. Coaches benched him because they feared he might get seriously injured, and they eventually cut him because they couldn't stand watching his talents go to waste. He lifted weights to develop his legs and upper body, but in the end it was a matter of physics, height meaning leverage and leverage meaning dominance. In the end, the skinniest lightweight forward could lean down on Tony and take his feet out from underneath him. And with their longer legs, taking three strides to Tony's five, opposing players beat Tony to the puck again and again.

By the time he was cut for good, he was mentally pre-pared for it, having suffered more than enough humiliation on the ice during games and in the locker room afterwards. To his surprise he was content to leave the physicality of the game behind, the actual playing of it against opponents so superior in size and speed. His regrets were not for the end of his playing, or in the humiliation of being bettered by players he outskilled by far, but in the lost potential for winning the Cup. He could always satisfy his desire to play the game at pickup and no-contact shinny games where size was not a factor and his timing and drive still made him a star. His ego could not suffer too much because he still was plainly better at the game than everyone he knew. But he would never win the Cup, not that cup, playing on concrete in July or at the Riverdale rink in mid-January.

On everyone's advice, he took to coaching, assisting his former mentors in forming the next generation of players after his own. He found, even, that he could occasionally teach his passion for defence, and he could pass on much of his skill to the hardest workers, but it was too difficult for him to watch the latest crop of non-growers like himself drift away to the bench and then to nowhere while less talented, less hardworking giants plowed their way to the top. He had no advice to give on how to get bigger when your body refused to do so, on how to change your genetic makeup so it included a bit more northern European tree trunk.

He switched to coaching girls hockey with its reduced emphasis on hitting and intimidation and its focus on pure speed and skill. But girls have their own reasons for never getting their hands on the Cup. Not even his lankiest, most acrobatic girl goalie, more catlike and instinctual than any boy he'd ever seen between the pipes, not even she would ever drink champagne from the Cup. The unfairness of it overwhelmed him and he gave up the job of building kids' impossible dreams for the amusement of others. He moved to the university leagues, coaching varsity girls' teams, girls who played only for fun and dreamed of medical or law degrees instead of trophies.

At the University of Toronto, he attended lectures in his off-hours and began to read widely, an experience so new to him it felt like travelling. He met, bedded, and was blissfully left by a visiting professor named Ewa Loest. He began to consider that there just might be something more than the winning of that particular cup involved in leading a fulfilling life. He began listening to baseball games and watching the birds in the trees around campus.

But his years in the hockey system in Toronto, and his skill with the stick had made him a lot of friends in the game. Through one of these friends, he was eventually offered a job with the League, in scheduling. It was a desk assignment plotting out the travel plans of all the boys who had managed to grow that extra four or five inches.

The next morning there was no answer from behind Fred's door. Tony slapped at the wood with an open palm and shouted his name. It occurred to him there were very few alternatives to Fred's hearse for moving both a body and a championship trophy back to Toronto. He could rent a minivan, but how would he get Stan inside it without all the casket-moving equipment hearses contain? He was relieved to find the young driver in the lobby restaurant. In the same clothes as the night before, the black silk suit and black cap of a hearse driver, Fred smelled of bar smoke and spilled wine. He was leaning heavily on one elbow and staring into a cup of black coffee. He smiled when Tony took the booth bench across from him. Though clearly exhausted, his eyes were shining.

"I don't regret a minute of it," he said. "Today, at around three, when we're fighting traffic back in Scarborough, I'm gonna feel about as bad as a man can feel, but I still won't regret it."

"You saw the sun come up?"

"Like a great big eyeball, man. Like a fucking big eyeball looking at me and winking, saying 'that's right, man, that's living.' The sun? Man that was hours ago. You know what I've seen since the sun came up, man?"

"What have you seen?"

When the sun had first slipped through the window that morning, it hit the Cup like some druidic prophecy. There were shine demons dancing on every wall, the ceiling and the floor. Tony lay in bed for over an hour watching the shifting play of light, the inexplicable colours. When he went to shower, he dragged the Cup along the carpet and stood it outside the bathroom, where he could see it from the glass stall.

"Man, I left the last club at around 4:30. That was over there on Saint-Denis just before it heads up the mountain, right near where we left buddy yesterday. I come walking out of the club ready to hit the sack, you know, and right there across the road is this strip club, and it's letting out too. Just the girls, no customers. I guess the customers got booted before that, so now it's just the girls kissing the doorman goodnight, laughing and giggling to themselves. No longer on the hunt, you know? Man. You know what strippers do when they're finished work at 4:30 in the morning?"

"Go to bed?"

"You'd think, wouldn't you? Not these girls. They get a look at me, and I guess it's the hat sets them off. Pretty goofy hat when it comes right down to it. They're all yelling and whistling to me across the street, and I'm pointing my finger at myself like Jerry Lewis, you know, like playing around all 'who, me?' and they're loving it. Next thing I know I'm up in some park past Sherbrooke there, smoking hash with three strippers and watching them dance to the sunrise. You know, them girls, even with their clothes on, they've got the moves. And there I am, just lying on the grass in this beautiful warm morning, my head full of hash, and all this beauty in my eyes."

"You still have your wallet?"

"No, I don't still have my wallet, but as I said, I don't regret a thing."

"Still have the keys to the hearse?"

"Yes, I do. Them girls wouldn't go near a hearse if you paid them. Very superstitious bunch, the erotic entertainment crowd."

"Who would have guessed?"

"You think they took my wallet, but you're wrong. These girls each make more in a night than you and I combined make in a week. What the fuck do they want my wallet for? I'd be more likely to steal from them."

Tony ordered an omelette for himself, a bagel and cream cheese for Fred, and more coffee. They had to be at the funeral home for ten, and he wanted to hit the highway as soon as possible after that. There was another funeral home waiting for Stan in Toronto, and the Cup was expected to make a trip to Florida at the end of the week. The office had gone into a frenzy at the news of Stan's death. There was no contingency in place, like everyone expected Stan to just keep doing his job forever.

The young driver straightened himself and leaned across the table, grabbing at Tony's arm. Clearly, the story of his night would continue, with or without Tony's co-operation.

"So then, I'm walking back along Sainte-Catherine's there, way over in the east end, and I've got three different kisses to think about, still on my mouth, you know. I can still feel that last one. I think they were all trying to outdo each other, you know, and she wins. Ouch. And I'm walking along—this is just a couple hours ago now. There's a few people on the street, the early workers, you know, picking up garbage and opening up the depanneurs, and it's like the greatest morning of my life all of a sudden, you know, all zoned on the hash and the sun shining, and suddenly there's this dog. It's like this big German shepherd thing with a yellow bandana around its neck, and it's limping around on the sidewalk in front of me, holding one of its front paws in the air. I can take a lot of things man. I mean, I move dead people around all day, right, but I can't take seeing a hurt dog. Breaks my heart to see a hurt dog."

During breakfast, the street outside the hotel, Boulevard René-Lévesque, filled with the morning rush, cars and buses and business people walking fast to their offices. Montreal's second face, the desperate, struggling centre of commerce, came out to replace the cooler, more relaxed Montreal of the night.

"And it belongs to this street kid, this girl with hair dyed all purple and shaved up the back and sides. You know, you see them all downtown these days; they live in the empty lots. A lot of them keep dogs, for protection I guess, or maybe they just like dogs. She's sitting off the sidewalk in this overgrown lot. I guess maybe that's where she lives, just her and her dog among the rocks that used to be a building."

"She took your wallet?"

Tony kept his involvement in the conversation minimal. The less he talked, the sooner it would be over. Stan had told him about this part of the job. "You're not really supposed to be there, so everyone gets uncomfortable and starts telling you the story of their fucking lives. After a while, you figure out where it's going, and you can try to nudge it there a bit faster."

"She won my wallet. I wanted to give her some money so she could take her dog to a vet or something, or at least buy some food for the thing, and for herself—something, but you can never tell where that money's going to go. I don't usually care about that. What someone on the street does with the money I give them, that's their own business, but there was a dog involved. I'm standing there, trying to tell her what to do with the ten bucks I just gave her and she's just smiling up at me. She can probably smell the hash and booze coming off me so who am I to give lectures at that point? But she sees that I have more than ten bucks in my wallet. That's when she offers to play me for the rest of my money."

"Play you?"

"She's got this plastic chessboard with her, keeps it set up all the time on one of the pieces of broken concrete. That's her thing, right. They've all got a thing. Hers is she'll play you chess for money. Jocelyn, that's the name she gives me. You put however much money down that you want to risk and if Jocelyn wins, she keeps it."

Fred looked out the window, took off his cap and scratched a shaky hand through his hair. The hair stood on end where the fingers left it.

"My guess is Jocelyn almost always wins," he said.

The restaurant was filling with other travellers, groups of older Americans in town on a tour. They sat in the seats surrounding Fred and Tony, wearing comfortable clothing, staring at Fred in his rumpled black suit.

"I know a little bit about chess. My uncle taught me when I was just a kid and I got really good at it for a while there. Won a bunch of tournaments at school and travelled around a bit with it. But this girl, man, she was a monster. You know chess? It's all about them four middle squares, right? Take control of them four middle squares and you're on your way. But this chick, man, she didn't give a shit about them four middle squares. She sees me setting up in the middle and she just laughs because she's already kicking my ass somewhere else."

"And you're still stoned at this point?"

"I know, I know, I thought the same thing. The first game I lost—twenty bucks—I figured it was probably because of the hash. And I didn't even mind losing the money because I wanted her dog to get to a vet. I was going to give her the money even if I won. I wanted her to feed the damn dog today, you know. So, I give my head a shake and play for all I've got left—another fifteen bucks.

"And this time I'm really watching, really paying attention to what it is she's doing, but you know, it's like she and I, we're not even playing the same game. I'm playing chess and she's playing this other game that makes chess look like tic-tac-toe. You know the best players in the world have entire games memorized, with thousands of variations to every move. If you make this move, say you bring out your bishop on the third move, that's standard, they look into their big box of games in their head and say okay, bishop out on the third move is when I throw my knight into the middle. Then let's say you try to mix it up a bit and bring out your queen. Unless it's an absolutely stupid move, they've already anticipated it, and they have three possible moves at their disposal to pick from.

"For these people, chess is a room with a thousand doors, each door leading into another room with a thousand doors, and on and on. And they always know which door is best. In their minds, there is a red carpet on the floor of each room, leading directly to the best possible door to the next room. You and I step into these rooms, all we see are doors, but these people have a red carpet. It's not really about being smarter than the other person. It's some kind of extra sense, like mind reading. There's this place out there, you know, in the air, where all the answers are, a place where the doors are marked with the red carpet, and if you can access that place, well there you are.

"That's what this chick was like. She'd make a move and then she'd sort of stare off into the street, looking after her dog, or just watching people go by until I made my move. And as soon as I made my move, you could see her seeing the right door. If you play the game to any competitive level, these are the people you eventually run into, the ones who let you know it's time to sit down; you've reached the end of your winning streak and now it's time to take your seat where you belong."

"So she won the second game as well?"

"She didn't win it. She owned it from beginning to end. These people don't win, they just are. You just don't expect to find one of them living on the street in Montreal, you know, begging food for their dog. Yeah, she took my fifteen bucks. Then she sees my wallet is empty and she gets this smile on her face, like she knows I'm a fighting fish and I'm not letting go of the hook. She smiles at me and says she'll play me for the wallet itself, and everything in it. If she wins, I can cancel my credit cards, but I have to give her a day before I do it. She's got it all figured out, so you know she's done this shit before. She gets a day to throw as much on the card as she can and I don't have to pay for it because I report it stolen. I just say I had my pocket picked and didn't notice it for a long time and the card company forgives me all the charges that aren't mine. They're insured for just this kind of delayed reporting, so it's all covered. Just a cost of doing business for those guys.

"And if I win, she says, I get whatever I want. I get all my money back, I get the dog if I want it; and if I want, I get her. She says she'll come back to my room with me if I win, if that's what I want. I'm still thinking of walking away, and she must know that because that's when she pulls out the blindfold. She's going to play the whole game without being able to see the board. I'm supposed to tell her my moves, and move her pieces for her when she decides on a move. This I've got to see, so I put my wallet down and she blind-folds herself. She plays the entire game looking only at a board in her head. She has to keep a picture of where every piece is on the board at all times. It's not impossible, but I've never seen it before, so we play."

"And that's when she took your wallet."

Fred gave Tony a weary look.

"Yeah, and that's when that happened. You know, I might just have brought her back to my room if I'd won. I might just have done that, because right now I'm thinking I'm in love with that girl. She beat my ass blindfolded."

Tony picked up the breakfast cheque, put it on the League's expense. He brought the Cup down to the parking garage.

Fred dozed in the driver's seat while Tony loaded it into the back of the hearse. On Ontario Street, two guys from the funeral home loaded Stan for them. A block from the highway entrance on René-Lévesque, Tony had Fred pull over and took charge of the wheel himself.

"You know, you need a special licence to drive one of these things, man."

"And right now, neither one of us could produce one. If we get pulled over, I'll just show the cop the Cup."

"That's one all-powerful cup you got there, man."

It was Tony's turn to shoot a tired look.

"Fred, *man*, I have to say, I'm not buying this line you keep handing me where you have no idea what's in that black case back there. I mean, we live in the same country, right? You're younger than me, but what difference does that make? You're telling me you've never heard of that trophy."

"What's your question? Have I heard of it, or do I care?"

"Yeah, that's what I thought."

"I mean, do you know what the international cricket trophy looks like? The Ashes—it's called the Ashes."

"Absolutely not, but that wasn't my point."

"Because about a billion more people care about that thing than about your shiny little cup back there."

"I'm aware of that."

"No offence buddy, but get your head out of your ass. Hockey is a money game."

"I can't argue against that."

"You know, when India plays Pakistan at cricket for the Ashes, people die. Did you know that?"

"I think I knew that."

"With all due respect, who gives a crap about your cup?"

Fred smiled the smile he'd learned from tired strippers that morning, threw his cap on the floor and climbed over the seatback to lie down beside Stan.

Tony drove the limit on the 401, a six-hour trip, with Stan's casket locked into the back, the Cup in its case on one side of him and Fred stretched out asleep on the other side. He stopped for gas in Brockville, coffee and a doughnut in Kingston. He was surprised to find a radio installed in the dashboard. It brought him a minor league baseball game from across the lake in New York somewhere, until it faded out in the crowded airwaves around Toronto. Somewhere, the Trojans were doing the unexpected and beating the Bulls by one run. Off the highway, on the crowded streets of Toronto, Tony woke Fred and let him drive the final few blocks to the funeral home where Stan would lie three days, visited by hockey players and League dignitaries, but no family or friends other than Tony, who showed up every day.

Eight

On his first overseas trip of the new off-season, during eight turbulent hours between Toronto and Italy, Tony sits in an aisle seat in first class beside the trophy. Across the aisle from him is Dragos Petrescu, the first Romanian-born hockey player to play on a Cup-winning team. He is flying to his homeland days after his family and friends have already arrived there. The promotions schedule for a new champion is making him very nearly late for his own wedding.

Beside Dragos, a young woman reads a book and glances now and then out the window. She is Diana Petrescu, the young player's cousin, also travelling to his wedding. Her mother, a sour looking woman dressed in black, snoozes in the window seat. Tony was introduced to them, and to Dragos's tall, imposing father in the first-class departures lounge in Toronto. He felt surrounded by family, and enjoyed the atmosphere while understanding almost nothing of what was being said around him, the group switching from Romanian to English so quickly here and again that all the words ran together unless someone spoke directly at him.

"My cousin is a very talented athlete," Diana had told

Tony, "but he could lose his own ass trying to get from one place to another. He has been known to show up at the airport twelve hours late for a flight. It's amazing to me he can find the ice whenever he falls off his skates."

Tony had watched Dragos submit himself to Diana's verbal abuse, and had wondered at his almost instant attraction to her because of it. "What a horrible girl," he'd thought, wanting her. She'd nagged her cousin until everyone was safely belted in, at which point she pulled out her book and treated the two of them like they had never existed for her. About the trophy she'd had only one thing to say. "You'll ruin your back in a job like that," she told Tony, as he heaved the bulky trophy case toward the boarding gate. "You'll be no good to anyone in a few years."

"My uncle has already called to tell me my picture has been in the Bucharest papers every day since the seventh game," Petrescu tells Tony. The jet has levelled off, the warning lights relaxed and the first round of drinks is being circulated through the cabin. "They've even published pictures of my fiancée. It feels very odd to return this way. It's not my first time back, of course, but I think it will be the first time I can't come back unnoticed."

"It bothers you, being noticed?" Tony asks.

"I don't know that it bothers me, Tony. It's not as though I am a player on the national soccer team. That would be trouble for me. Those guys can't take a drink of water without people fighting for the glass afterwards. I think it will be odd to return this way, that's all, especially considering how it was that I left Romania."

"Kicked out for sucking too much blood?" Tony smiles at the younger man.

"A joke about Dracula. That's good, Tony. I've never heard anything like it."

Tony lifts his glass of orange juice to Petrescu, toasting the successful sarcasm.

"Does Canadian hockey mean anything in Romania?" he asks.

"It's a game. That's what means something. I won a very important game, and to Romanians being the best at any game is what matters the most."

The young hockey player's father sits on the other side of the Cup, in the window seat of Tony's row. On his chin he wears a manicured goatee, midway in its transition from black to grey. In the airport he had not said a word in English, had never addressed Tony, but now he leans across the trophy and looks Tony in the eye.

"Romanians are masters of all games," he says, slowly and with a growing smile. He waves down a passing steward and orders his first of many transatlantic drinks. "I am master of all games."

When he says this, Diana sighs loudly and closes her book.

"Master of all games," she repeats, rolling her eyes. "That's good, Miki, play the foreigner for our new friend. You know, we're in an Italian airplane, and soon we'll be over the ocean. Who gets to play the exotic foreigner then?" She leans her body forward a few inches and addresses Tony. "He works for a department store in Montreal. He is a master of noth-ing. He is a master of talking about being a master."

There is a brief exchange between everyone in Romanian. It is not in the least heated, more bored than anything else, and at the end of it, Diana sighs again and pulls a silky black mask from her seat pocket. She fits it on her eyes, pulls a blanket up over her shoulders from her knees and collapses sideways against her mother's shoulder. Dragos watches her and makes an attempt to adjust the blanket for her, to bring it more securely over one shoulder. She bats his hand away blindly and says something decidedly affectionate. The two of them laugh, and Dragos turns back to Tony.

"For me," the older man begins again, "the very act of living is the playing of a game against the greatest opponent. So, we meet then. I am Nicolae Petrescu-Nicolae. Call me Miki. Everyone does."

"That's a lot of Nicolaes."

"Everyone of a certain generation in Romania has Nicolae somewhere in their name. We are also lucky enough to have it also as a family name, though. Some, like my son, have chosen to use only the first last name. It makes it easier to fit on his hockey sweater. This is what he says."

Tony hears a bitterness in Petrescu's voice he didn't expect. He looks across the aisle at Dragos, who is listening while pretending not to. Not for the first time he notices the young player is fidgeting almost uncontrollably with his hands. Tony had seen this nervous habit in the departures lounge as well. Dragos Petrescu is clearly agitated by the flight, as though the return to Romania terrifies him in some way.

"And do you expect to win the game," Tony asks the older man, "you know, the game of living?"

"One always expects to win. For me, life is playing. Everything, every game, even the most serious, the most full of consequence can be contested. Perhaps if I'd had more of a choice, my son would not have satisfied his father so well

JOHN DEGEN

by becoming excellent at his own game. But he is very good at hockey. What can he do about it? Are you very good at anything, Tony?"

Tony takes a slow sip of his own traditional flying drink, double rye and ginger ale, and looks past Nicolae to the dense blackness of the night outside the window.

"So, how did you come to leave Romania?" Tony asks. Across the aisle, the masked Diana sighs heavily again and shifts in her seat.

To enter Israel when Nicolae Petrescu-Nicolae did, and more importantly how he did, with a young wife of working age and a son not too many years away from mandatory service in the army, was to be certain of a very difficult time. His visa to leave Romania depended on his being Jewish, but in fact he was not Jewish.

His mother was Jewish by birth but not practice and Nicolae, having been born into the great socialist republic of Romania was officially without religion. But a Jewish mother is a Jewish mother and that made him officially a Jew in the eyes of Israel, which meant he received a visa for himself and for his non-Jewish wife and non-Jewish son. Nicolae and his family were permitted to take very little with them, as there was really no such thing as personal property in the Romania of the day, and even family heirlooms were considered to be cultural treasures of the Revolution.

In the months before their departure, Nicolae was regularly removed from the street by the police and taken to the station for questioning. Every neighbourhood in Bucharest had its own station, responsible for its own small district and population. Nicolae was well acquainted with his local police station from his days as a juvenile delinquent, but this was something different entirely. This was the central station, off Victory Square. This was the home of the state police. Securitate. Invisible men. Nicolae was removed from the street, he was told, for being publicly drunk.

"It is certainly true I was publicly drunk," Petrescu laughs, "though I doubt they could actually tell. I can drink an entire bottle of vodka and look as fresh as though I'd just had a cup of coffee. Drunkenness was simply the easiest and most common excuse for arrest and detainment."

Until his departure from Romania, Nicolae still attended his job every day, though he felt very little reason to continue doing work. Many of his very good friends worked with him, and as they were all upset that he would soon be leaving, they made it a point to get him drunk each day before three in the afternoon. So it was that every day of his last months in Bucharest, Nicolae walked home from work completely without legs, and so it was on many of these days he found himself spending some time with the dreaded secret police.

On the first of his series of detainments, Nicolae was placed alone in a large dark room on an upper floor of the downtown station. He had been made to climb at least five flights of stairs, though he couldn't be sure because of his condition. On his way up the stairs he had concentrated on sounds. There were stories of the unmistakable noise of torture coming through the walls of this station, but all Nicolae heard was the mechanical hum of the ventilation system and the occasional cough or laugh from behind a closed door. The two Securitate pushed him into a hard wooden chair beside a large table, and then left the room. While they were gone, Nicolae twisted in the chair and observed his darkened surroundings.

The room was mostly bare, no wall decor, no windows, just the large wooden table like something designed for feasts or large meetings, and seven identical wooden chairs with no padding on the seats. When he looked down at his own chair he saw markings in the back rails near the seat, dents and rubbing marks, like those made by handcuffs or chains. Nicolae wiped the palms of his hands on his pant legs to remove the sweat that was accumulating there. In one murky corner of the room there was a dark shape, something hulking or piled. Nicolae stood from his chair and took a few tentative steps into the gloom. He expected at any moment for a voice to stop him and leave him sweating and silent on his feet, but the only sound he heard was from his own shoe soles dragging across the wooden floor. As he approached the corner, he found himself laughing low and uncontrolled. There was a small table, a folding table like he himself used for playing bridge with friends, and on the tabletop was a backgammon game, set for fresh play.

Nicolae taps his forehead with a finger. "You could never tell in a police station in Bucharest if what you were seeing at any moment was really what was there, or just something constructed for you to see and wonder about. The police station was a house of games. Games of the mind. Not such nice games like we play."

The backgammon set was in the same place each time Nicolae was brought into the room. He never saw anyone playing it nor any evidence of play. He imagined the police must have played it on their lunchtime, or in the morning before it was time to interrogate. It looked foreign, not the table sets you would normally see in Romania. It was made of something heavy, like marble or even a slab of steel, and the pieces were actual stones. In Romania, one almost always played table sets from the mountains of Transylvania. Peasants in the mountains would construct wooden box sets out of a light wood, bass or pine—quite thin and with little heft. They would include quick, rural carvings on the outside of the boxes, and the pieces were nothing more than round wooden chips painted red or black.

But the game in the station was something else entirely, an alien-looking thing, something confiscated perhaps. At that time in Romania, in the late 1970s, it was possible to travel from Romania if you knew the right people and had the right job—if you were in, or connected to, the Party. And everyone who travelled brought back some little thing, sometimes many little things. There was always something tucked away in the suitcase. At the border it was only a matter of packing cigarettes, a small cheese or fine chocolates on the very top of the suitcase, some small gift for the border guards, and everything else in the case made it through safely. It was a game in itself to discover the desires of certain border guards.

The very best players at contraband kept lists of the likes and dislikes of all the customs men at Otopeni Airport, and at the rail borders. They kept work schedules and knew when vacations were due. In this way, they could be certain of who would be greeting them on their return to Romania, and what little token to pack on the top of the clothes in the suitcase. Nicolae knew of one fellow who had no interest in the traditional bribes—the cigarettes, cigars, cheeses or chocolates. And he wanted nothing for a woman. He was a very successful bachelor and never had to bother with winning the attentions of ladies. All this man wanted was fishing tackle.

This particular border guard fished in every spare moment. When he was not at Otopeni, opening the suitcases of visiting dignitaries, thumbing through their underwear for state secrets, he was at one of the many lakes in Bucharest. He fished for carp, mostly, and also brown trout, though these were quite rare in the city. To get past this man was a simple matter of visiting a sporting goods store on your travels and picking up the most extravagant and ridiculous looking piece of fishing tackle you could find. You would do well to buy some spare fishing line as well, and a few plain hooks; but some colourful piece of fish silliness was a certain free pass back into the country. Something from Finland was best, shaped like a fish and painted like no fish in nature, something with feathers and beads and parts that flutter or twirl in the water.

"I'm not sure if this man ever used any of this crazy Finnish tackle—he was always just as pleased to see the line and plain hooks—but he was certainly amused by it."

In fact, this guard's crazy foreign fishing tackle fed that significant and mysterious national pride all border officials seem to possess. He looked at these strange and wonderful lures as evidence of Western decadence and the futility of the capitalist system. "Look at this ridiculous contraption," he could be heard to say. "What self-respecting fish would ever try to eat this thing with its feathers and beads and funny noises? Maybe Finnish fish need to be amused before they are caught, but a good Romanian carp wants just a bug on a hook." Nevertheless, an absurd Finnish piece of tackle, some cheap line and plain hooks cleared the path for, no doubt, hundreds of kilos of contraband chocolate from Geneva, or cigars from Amsterdam, Camembert from Paris, or prosciutto from Rome.

Perhaps they even cleared the path for a strange table set made of a metal slab with stones for pieces. Stranger things were brought into Romania in the suitcases of those privileged few who could cross borders with ease. Perhaps this game that haunted Nicolae belonged to an official who was eventually discredited, and it was then confiscated from his apartment along with all his wife's underwear, the television and any good food he had stashed away in the cupboards.

"You are getting a sense of how things worked in Romania, yes?" Nicolae smiles a sad smile and takes a drink from his small bottle of beer. "Probably how things still work if I am right, but who knows? It is no longer my concern. I am no longer Romanian. Now I am a Canadian immigrant from Israel. Nothing to do with Romania any more, except when it is time to return and witness my son getting married."

Possibly, the police stole some poor man's handmade table set before they put him in a secret camp to spend a few years doing the laundry of hundreds of criminals. It's entirely possible they didn't even know how to play backgammon, these two policemen who possessed such a fine and mysterious set. But there were games they did play very well. Because Nicolae's father was in the Party when it meant something to be in the party, Nicolae had, in fact, little to fear from the regular police. The Securitate were a different matter, but drunk as he was and with a visa in his pocket he chose to ignore the danger.

As young men, Nicolae and his friends would go out into the city at night, walking the streets long past curfew, and crossing into different police zones. They didn't care. They could run fast—they all played handball, some on the under-19 national team, and had the legs of young athletes. Not too many policemen, fat or otherwise, were any match for them on open ground, especially with all the fences to jump and gardens in which to hide. Occasionally, the boys had too much to drink and didn't see the police coming until it was too late. The police played a trick they favoured, approaching curfew breakers in a car without lights on. They would wait until the car was right beside the young drunks, and then they would switch on their headlights and turn across the road to stop them. It was a ridiculous sort of ruse because as soon as the boys noticed a car approaching without lights on, they knew it was the police and away they would go on their legs. But sometimes drunk beyond all sense, and singing, they didn't hear the car approaching. The trick worked well enough on those occasions.

With these young sons of privilege, interaction with police after curfew was little more than a warning, the playing of a game about power. The police wanted the boys to understand that state authority had some control over them, even them, national-level athletes and the sons of Party members. In fact, each side played a little game at night in the quiet streets of Bucharest, both the drunk young men and the police. If the officers suspected the boys were well-connected, and they would have to be to be engaged in such risky behaviour, the police would hold off asking them for identity papers for as long as possible. In that way, they could treat the boys a bit more roughly for a short time. They could push them against the wall and shine torches into their faces. They could order them to be quiet and tap the barrels of their weapons to let them know they meant business. All this the police could do until they discovered who the young men were, but after, they would have to be more polite. So, for the bored and proud officers, there was great advantage in not immediately knowing the names of the drunks they stopped in the streets. And for Nicolae and his friends as well, it was amusing not to volunteer too much information too quickly. Later, of course, Nicolae would not believe dealings with the police were so amusing, but at the time he was just a foolish adolescent with too much time and too little responsibility. He enjoyed the late-night interactions. He especially enjoyed the running away, because he had the young athlete's pure love of running. There was a coolness and a moisture to the air of the city when he was running, a brilliance, and his legs sprang so effortlessly off the stone streets.

The interrogations were amusing as well. It was a little dance they all did at those times, the police shoving the boys around and not asking for their papers until they could think of nothing else to do, and Nicolae and his friends being shoved around, protesting, giggling, attempting, each individually, to walk away while someone else was being questioned. One of the boys, a fearless drunk named Paul, would wait until one of his friends had said something particularly stupid to the officers, making them angry. It was not difficult to make these men angry in the middle of the night. These men were very sensitive to insult, and seemed, in particular, always on the watch for an intellectual slight. The young men knew from experience the favourite question of the police was, "Do you think we are not intelligent?" or some variation—"Do you think we did not also go to school? Do you think you are the only ones who have read the great Russian writers?"

This response often came after Nicolae had used a favourite excuse: "We're very sorry comrade officers, but we have been left in charge of a visiting Russian student, a Comrade Raskolnikov, and he has wandered off and become lost."

The police were concerned that the boys understood how they were not inferiors. Yet the truth, sadly for them, was that in the great People's Republic, in which the lowest was the highest and the very concept of social strata was meant to dissolve, it was still possible for the people's guard to be inferior to stupid, arrogant sons of the Party.

"Ideals are wonderful things, yes, but they rarely transcend the baser human tendencies of envy and jealousy and pride." Nicolae rubs his eyes and smiles shyly. "Even in bad times, people have the opportunity to act badly. It is shameful, but true."

The other boys would get the guards talking angrily to one of them in particular, asking their questions, trying to work out whether or not they were insulting him, and Paul would just walk off. His best trick was to slip into the darkness, run a little way down the road and then walk back toward the group, whistling loudly. This drove the police into fits of authority. Paul would come walking back, acting sober but whistling too loudly, and when the police would tell him to get back against the wall, he would play as though he'd never seen the rest of the group in his life. *But Com-*

rade Officer, I don't know these young criminals at all. You've
mistaken me, I was just returning from visiting my girlfriend.
I know it is past the curfew, but you understand how women
are. When they want it, they want it, and besides, her husband
works with you fellows and so is only out at night.

This was really taking things too far, but they were so
arrogant, so sure of their positions. Still, the boys paid for
it with the odd poke of a nightstick into the ribs, or even
sometimes a knee to the groin. It was all just part of the
game. Paul suffered on that particular night. He should not
have brought wives into it, but he liked to push past the
boundaries. He went home with a split lip that night, and a
warning not to tell his father how it happened.

That was how it almost always ended. Eventually the
police would feel the need to move on and they'd ask for
identity papers. Then, on recording names and addresses—
addresses they could not help but understand to be those of
Party members—they let the boys go with a lecture about
responsibility to the state, and the pleasures of not climbing
above the general rights of the people for whom the state
was originally formed. It would almost always end with
false friendliness on both sides, a sort of smiling, winking
agreement that a game had been well-played that evening,
and until we all meet again.

But there was to be no *until we meet again* when Nicolae was leaving Romania for good. He discovered then
that connections in the Party mean very little for admitted
traitors to the republic. It took him two years to secure a
visa for himself and another year to get visas for his wife
and child.

"It was very painful for Dragos's grandfather," Petrescu

explains, "because he was a proud Communist—he is a proud Communist to this day. You will meet him as well. He could not understand his son's need to leave the country, his need to drag half the family from the bosom of their country, even when it was at its worst in the years immediately before 1989."

In those later years just before the Revolution, Nicolae's father, Razvan Petrescu, managed to be grateful his son and grandson were safely in North America, though it hurt him to know it was their preference, and that they would not be returning to help rebuild the country. But the three years before Nicolae left were terrible for the old man. It was never a secret when someone applied for a visa to emigrate. This information travelled quickly and did swift damage. Where before, his father had walked confidently into his office as Razvan Petrescu, Secretary to the Lithographers Union and original Party member (both Dragos Petrescu's grandfather and grandmother, Nicolae's mother and father, were imprisoned by the Nazis for being members of the Communist Party) suddenly he was "that Petrescu" whose son is stealing from the people by fleeing the country in a time of great need.

The moment Nicolae asked for a visa application at the government office, a special file was opened on him at the police station downtown. And if there was a file for him, there was a file for every member of his family, including his proud Communist parents. To be watched and followed and paid special attention to meant very little to Nicolae, but it was a great and painful shame to his father. It meant large, ugly men in overcoats came to his office and asked his staff questions about him, about what time he came in every morning and when he left in the evenings; if he met with any suspicious-looking people on a regular basis; if perhaps he was having an affair with some young girl who might be an agent of counter-revolution. These men spread rumours about him that had no basis in fact, but which were the standard rumours you always heard about people with family who had left—that their connection to the decadent, Western world had weakened their communist values, and that they had been turned into moles for an eventual capitalistic overthrow. There was a sudden shift of power between old Razvan and the people who worked for him—his authority was destroyed by a thousand whispers and unending lunchtime gossip.

Nicolae had his own troubles to deal with in those three years. Everything became more difficult. Lines stretched longer; it was no longer possible to sweet-talk the woman behind the deli counter in order to get the secret Hungarian salami stashed out of sight beneath the terrible Romanian stuff. Why should she do favours for Nicolae, who was leaving her and the rest of his Romanian family—all the country, one large family—to go and live in Hollywood?

"This always is what we heard," Nicolae laughs, "that all emigrants were going to go and live in Hollywood. As though this was the only choice. Who the hell would go and live in Hollywood? Yet this was always the accusation."

Really, Nicolae was taking his young family to Israel to nearly starve to death over two long years before they found their way to Canada and some comfort and freedom, finally. Nicolae had his troubles. He had a police escort to deal with. Being the son of an original Party member made his leaving that much worse for the state, that much more embarrassing, so some effort was made to make it extra hard on him.

"Perhaps they thought they could change my mind through these intimidations. Perhaps it was like a parent trying to scare his child into behaving, all for his own good." Nicolae looks at Tony and tips the small empty bottle above his lap, twisting his face in a look of exaggerated pain at its emptiness. He presses the button on his armrest to call an attendant. "But, of course, the more you challenge me, the more I look for my own advantage."

If you walk just beyond the small suburban settlements around Bet She'an in Israel, where Nicolae Petrescu-Nicolae settled with his young family in 1984, you will reach the neatly laid-out groves of blood oranges. There the fruit hangs white from the branches, powdered over completely with a chemical to resist disease and kill insects. The farmers there send dogs to run the fence line and stop those who would pick the fruit without permission. Without the dogs it would be possible to do this, as the plantations are large and widespread. There are high fences of twisted wire, but with holes wide enough to reach an arm through. Therefore, the dogs. To get the fruit, then, it would be necessary to understand the dogs, either to know when they are away from the fences, or to discover what it is that wins their trust. With all animals there is a key to trust; some posture you can take or something you can give them that will get behind their instinct. Nicolae was determined to find this key.

The mistake the farmers made was to release only one dog in each grove. Several dogs and Nicolae would not have been so effective in his thievery, because as he worked on one dog the others would have been at his throat. His technique, and he was quite proud of it, was to confuse the dog. When the dog arrived at the fence and Nicolae was there, it thought it knew the situation. Nicolae was there to take the oranges, and the dog was to stop him. To confuse his foe Nicolae did not take the oranges. Instead, for one week, he just stood and looked at the dog while it barked at him, while it threw the full weight of its huge silver-grey body onto the fence. Nicolae stood at a safe distance, looked at it and smiled. He did not try to speak to it, or approach it. He simply made the dog think twice about why he might be there. He looked at it, and then he picked up his briefcase and walked away.

For three days, it followed him along the fence, snarling and spitting, as he walked away, but on the third day as soon as Nicolae walked away, the dog just stood and watched him go, satisfied with the pattern of things. On the second week, Nicolae made a move on the dog. He had thought to wait until it would not bark at the sight of him, but then decided it would be better the other way. To make a move on the dog while it was barking would confuse the animal more than to do so while it was still. So, one day on the second week, while the dog barked at him, Nicolae walked over to the fence and thrust his arms through. He did not move suddenly, or make any noises. He just strode with purpose to the fence and put his arms through the wide holes. The dog was indeed surprised and, according to the plan, very confused. Nicolae grabbed the dog by the collar and closed his fists tight into the struggling animal's neck. In this way he kept the dog from twisting his head far enough to either side to bite into an arm or hand. He let the snarling beast twist a little, in order to allow him to smell his attacker's flesh on him, and even taste it a little with his lolling tongue, but no biting. In this way, Nicolae held onto the dog for one half-hour exactly.

At first it was very difficult to hold the dog as it pulled away from the fence and was very strong in the back legs. The dog jumped and twisted in its desperate need to bite into Nicolae's arms.

"At one point the dog began to piss through the fence at me," Nicolae says, shaking his head. "I am not sure if the dog actually wanted to do this or if it merely released because of fear. But I stood there and held the dog by the neck as it pissed hard onto my pant legs. All the while I looked at the dog in the same manner as before. Made eye contact and just looked with concentration, and as little fear as possible. Then, after half an hour, I let go of the dog and stepped back from the fence. At this point, I had won. The dog did not bark. Instead it dropped its nose to the ground and looked up at me. Confused, you see. And that is when I picked up my briefcase and walked away."

For the next three days the dog received the same treatment. A quick determined lunge from Nicolae and half an hour of confused twisting. It pissed again only once, and by the third day the dog was waiting for Nicolae to lunge through the fence. It wanted Nicolae to lunge through the fence. The lunging had become a game to the dog. The dog still would have liked to bite into his arm—he had not removed this instinct from it, but the struggle with Nicolae was no longer a life-and-death struggle for the dog. It knew that after some time, Nicolae would eventually let go, pick up his briefcase and walk away. Now when it was time for him to leave, the animal was disappointed. Nicolae had completely confused its purpose. The dog was supposed to drive him from the fence and the oranges; now, instead, it wished he would stay.

By the end of the second week, Nicolae was able to do what he pleased on his own side of the fence and the dog merely sat and watched, waiting for arms to come through, for the game to begin. With the dog thus pacified, Nicolae was able to put his feet into the holes in the twisted wire and climb to the upper branches of the orange trees for the best fruit. He was able to gather as many oranges as would fit in his briefcase each day, and walk them out of the grove past the fence, and past the now docile, whimpering and thoroughly confused dog. Had he fallen into the dog's territory, no doubt the animal would have been at Nicolae's throat, and therefore he was very careful not to fall. In this way, Nicolae provided his family with fresh fruit, which was so important to them in that early time of their immigration when money was very scarce.

In Ostia, near Rome, there is a five-hour wait in the airport. A crowded bus on the tarmac and customs men with cigarettes hanging from their lips. There was a weird light effect during landing. It was how Tony first realized they were very near the ground. The right-hand windows began to flicker and a soft bank on the way in revealed the Mediterranean, unsettled, bouncing sunlight off a million waves, inviting. Diana's mother began again picking at the rosary she had put away an hour out of Toronto. Someone in coach was singing. Tony watched a man reach across the aisle to hand a large ring-shaped loaf of bread to a woman. Across from him, Dragos and his beautiful cousin checked their tickets and spoke with low tones in Romanian.

On the way over, it had felt like a vacation. Everyone on their way somewhere new. Tony had listened to Nicolae's endless stories of himself as he might watch an inflight movie, with as much or as little concentration as the moment required. A couple near them was beginning their honeymoon and couldn't stop kissing each other. When they thought no one was looking the man would slip his hand into his new wife's blouse, and she would lean in, her hand disappearing between his legs. From overheard pieces of their conversation Tony learned the newlyweds would make a brief stop in Rome to change planes and then continue on to Greece for two weeks on an island. They read and slept and kissed and laughed for eight hours across the ocean. Tony watched them when the movie was boring, and they ignored him.

Now, for Tony and the four Petrescus, it is five hours of waiting in the sunny airport, beside the gate for the last leg of their flight, and already they are surrounded by Romanians. Now everyone is going home. Now the vacations are over. It is time to return for business or to bury someone. Time to bring money and chocolate and toys.

Tony keeps the trophy with him at all times. In airports he pushes it around on a cart, his own personal luggage bungeed on top of it to increase its disguise. Not that he imagines anyone here would recognize it, or care. For five hours he pushes the trophy around the terminal. He looks out of as many windows as he can find. Wall-sized panes of glass that curve overtop of him and let him see more of Italy than he'd expected to.

From one he watches other planes banking in low over the Mediterranean, though he can no longer see any water. He recognizes the play of light on their undersides. He thinks of Italian pilots smiling to each other as they slide back home over their own personal warm blue sea. Hands warmly slapping shoulders and cuffing the backs of heads. He thinks of clams in tomato sauce, and smells the cigarettes of customs officers and security guards. Twice he is stopped by young men with machine guns and dogs. German shepherds on thick leather leads, low-hipped and snarling, and the young men smoking, tapping their fingertips on the long pocked gun barrels. He is made to stand aside while the dogs circle his cart, sniffing the seams of the trophy case. He hopes the young men won't make him open the case. He believes he understands some words. The guards debating which musical instrument it might be. He stands to the side and smiles, staring out one of the tall windows, hoping the men and dogs will all go away from him.

Near the gate, it is all Romanians. Later, closer to boarding, they will be joined by Italian businessmen, dark-suited and hurried, but for this time, for five hours, this particular gate is part of Romania. They have all been there before. Have all bought cognac and American cigarettes in the duty-free, slept on benches, waited an endless five hours for the two-hour flight home.

"This is what one gets for living in an unimportant country." These are Dragos's first words to him since leaving the plane. "I've known it my entire life. Germans, Russians, French, Italians—they all fly. Romanians wait to fly."

Tony wonders if it is possible for a man to physically shrink on his way home. In an Italian airport, the hockey player's famous largeness looks like a bad magician's trick.

"Tony, I would like to drink."

"So drink," Tony says.

In a far terminal, at the end of long glass hallways, carpeted to hide the noise of a thousand luggage carts, Tony watches a lightning storm far out at sea. It is the best window he'll find. He watches shuttle buses pull away and circle down a long on-ramp to the highway leading to Rome. He watches tall grass lean back from the asphalt as the buses speed by. There are ruins in the centre of the turnpike. One low stone wall and stone lines of foundation, many rooms, all fenced in by metal spikes and yellow nylon rope. On all sides of it, fresh smooth roadway slides bus after bus of tourists on and off the highway.

Past the ruins the land drops off to a rocky beach. The sea finishes it, pale then, reflecting a sky that has clouded since they arrived. And in one small part of his view, far out to sea, lightning reaches down. Tony leans on the trophy's case and watches the storm blow itself out. This is where Diana finds him. She has been dividing the hours between the café and the duty-free shop. She carries a small paper bag with her.

"So, you are showing your girlfriend the sights of Italy, yes?" she says, without using his name. Tony pulls his gaze back from the Roman sky and takes her in. She looks tired from the travelling, her clothes rumpled and possibly too hot, her hair disarranged by static and lack of care. Nevertheless, he likes to look at her.

"Careful, Tony, she'll get jealous if you stare at another

woman." She stifles a quiet laugh.

"Who are you talking about?"

"This…" she taps the trophy case, "this love of your life. I've never seen such devotion. I think you must even talk to her when no one is looking. Do you talk to her as well, Tony? Does she understand you, like a good woman should?"

"It's just a job. I'm just doing what's expected of me. If I lost the trophy, I'd lose the job."

"So," she presses, pushing at a corner of the black case with her index finger, "if you left the case with the airline to take care of, this would not be good enough?"

"Airlines lose luggage. It happens every day. What would be the point of me arriving in Romania for the wedding, and the trophy arriving in Hong Kong? There is no point at all me going anywhere without this trophy. I'm not taking it to your cousin's wedding; it's taking me."

"That's what I say as well. You are her date—and what a sad thing to say, no point you going anywhere without it. You mean you never travel without it?"

"I just mean it's my job. When you travel for your job, travel is work."

"So what do you do for fun—for vacation?"

"I stay in one place. I sit still. I don't move."

"Hmmm. You and your girlfriend." She jabs at him now with her index finger. He feels the sharp crescent of her fingernail through the cloth of his sleeve. "You are made for each other."

"What's in the bag?'

"Sugar," she says. "Not sugar… the other kind, the fake one. Fake sugar packets." She opens the bag and shows Tony hundreds of pink and blue envelopes of synthetic sweetener. "I picked them up from the café. My grandfather is diabetic, and these are very hard to get in Romania. When I see them, I take them."

"You steal sugar packets wherever you go. You steal fake sugar."

"Yes," she says, nodding her head in mock disgust. "I am a thief, a pathetic immigrant. I also take those very soft paper napkins. Half of my suitcase is sugar packets and napkins. Do you know what paper napkins feel like in Romania? There are no paper napkins in Romania, that's what they feel like. They feel like nothing because they don't exist."

"No paper napkins," Tony repeats. "I had no idea your childhood was so horrible. You must be so happy every day you wake up in Canada, knowing you can wipe the corners of your mouth with paper."

"Delirious," she says flatly. She stares at Tony's face for a long time. Long enough to make him uncomfortable. He turns his eyes from her and watches a tourist bus drive off from the terminal.

"You are ugly," she says. "Not very handsome at all. But you are ugly in a different way from most Romanian men. It's an attractive sort of ugliness. Still, I can see why this is your only girlfriend."

"Okay." Tony nods slowly, his eyes dropping to the carpet. "I'm sorry I said the thing about the napkins. I'm sorry. I don't know shit about your country or about you."

"You don't know shit about anything, Tony." Diana smiles at him and lifts his chin with her finger. "But I'll say again, it is an attractive ugliness."

By the time they return to the gate, the businessmen are gathering. Petrescu stands seventh in line for boarding, beside his father and aunt. In his oversized suit, he might be fifteen.

After everyone has boarded, there is another delay. The pilot himself comes back into the cabin to ask about the Cup. He has heard of it; wants to touch it. Tony unstraps the seat belt and cracks the case. The pilot leans over Tony's seat. His hand disappears to the wrist.

"Like a woman," he says, and Diana giggles. "Like the hip of a beautiful woman." And then he laughs himself.

Tony wonders what it must mean to this man to fly planes. He looks at his forearms and wonders about electrical impulses, the instincts those arms have that his do not. The pilot shakes his hand then, and Tony squeezes, thinking about lift and drag.

"Have you kissed it?" the pilot asks, smiling. "It is like a woman. Surely you have kissed it."

"You have to win it to kiss it," Tony says. "Otherwise, what would be the point?"

They all laugh then. One of the businessmen from across the aisle speaks to an attendant in an annoyed voice. The pilot shakes his head and says something too softly to be heard. His eyes widen when he looks back at Tony.

"Still, I would like to kiss it."

Tony climbs out of his seat and moves back down the aisle to give the young pilot access. He knows the plane will go nowhere until he does. Tony is unable to see the kiss because there are too many bodies in the way, but he knows when it happens because there is cheering all around. On his way back to the cockpit, the pilot shakes Petrescu's hand

and then kisses him on the forehead.

"You have won her, yes?"

Petrescu nods. The pilot kisses his forehead again.

"For luck," he says.

In the air, Petrescu leans toward Tony and smiles.

"If it had been for soccer," he says, "we'd still be on the ground."

Around them, dark-suited businessmen snap their newspaper pages. Within two hours, they are circling Bucharest. From his window, Tony cannot get a sense of the city below. There are trees and lakes, but very few roads. He leans over the trophy case and stares at the ground below them. They circle the city several times, reluctant to land. Tony begins to wonder what the delay might be. He shifts in his seat and looks around for an attendant. Across the aisle, he hears Diana mumble in a half-sleep.

"Tony, don't worry. Probably, there is a dog on the runway." She is looking at him tiredly from just above the lip of her blanket, and he can tell from her eyes that she is smiling. "In Romania, there are no paper napkins, very little fake sugar, and dogs run wild at the airport. Welcome to my childhood."

Nine

Antonio Esposito Chiello, the keeper of the Cup, is sent to Romania in only his second full year on the job. It is a job passed on to him by death, a job he tries not to think about very much because he loves it too strongly to consider it real. Real, it might somehow go away. Other things, loved things, made real, had gone away. They always do.

In his new job, Tony practises a new way of working. He breathes; he looks around; he tries to interest himself in where he is and what there is to see and remember outside of the fact that he is there with the Cup. He refuses to think of the trophy as his responsibility, something to be taken care of. Instead, it is simply part of everything he sees and everywhere he goes. It is attached to his experience of everything, attached to him. For him, the trophy is just another arm.

Tony travels for three months every summer with three arms. He can lose sight of the Cup only as easily as he might lose sight of his own flesh. To leave it behind, he would first have to cut it away. It isn't there to be watched and looked after; it is simply there, part of Tony wherever he goes. And he goes wherever the League tells him to go. He asks no questions and makes no suggestions or complaints. He has learned all this from his old friend Stan.

There had been thoughts of winning the Cup. Early thoughts, like those of everyone else he knew. Born in Toronto in 1965, Tony had, in a way, already won the Cup twice, but as a child he had no memory of the celebrations. He knew the significance of his middle name, and understood why it was there like that. He wondered sometimes, "Why name me after a *Chicago* goalie?" but it was clear that for Tony's family being Italian was more important than being from either Toronto or Chicago. He remembered his father's friends at the house on Saturday evenings. Beer spilled into orange shag carpet. His mother laughing at him when he skated toward her across the backyard.

He remembered feeling no pressure, as though the winning of the Cup was there for him in his future, unquestionably. It would be done, and the way it would be done was by simply living a life the way he was living it. Posters on the wall, a bed held off the ground by four hockey pucks, a slice of oozing honeycomb in his mouth for the drive to the arena.

Coaches and referees praised him for his speed. His parents smiled at him from three rows above the glass. He grew and waited for time to bring him what he deserved. In the summer, he swam at Riverdale Pool during the hot days and played ball hockey on Grandview Avenue into the evenings. Things happened in his family. His father changed jobs every once in a while. The family sat at the kitchen table and his father would explain what the new job was all about. Where it was, how long the drive would be, when he would be home in the evenings, what kind of free stuff he could get. Always it seemed to be a better job. His mother smiled and laughed and made them all drink wine in fancy red-stained glasses.

His sister married a Scottish boy from the neighbourhood. There were three days of flowers and large meals. His father took pictures of everybody in the backyard, by the fence, in front of the roses. Antonio danced with his sister and she lifted him off the ground, kissing him and calling him her little Tony Esposito, her little goalie. There was endless cake.

Sometimes, his parents would bring another child home from the hospital. Twice it was sisters and the last was a brother. All of their cribs were held off the ground by four hockey pucks.

"That way," his father told Antonio, "the legs won't dent the carpet."

Twice a year, his father would take him to the game with tickets he got from someone at work. Antonio sat watching the players while his father walked from section to section, looking for better seats. Only once, he managed to sneak Antonio into the Golds. His father lifted him from the tunnel into the only available seat, beside a young woman and her date. He told Antonio to watch out for him across the ice, and then disappeared back into the tunnel. A little later, the girl tapped Antonio on the leg, smiled, and pointed out his father to him, across the ice in the Greys, waving both arms. When Toronto scored, the girl gripped Antonio's leg with her long fingernails and bounced on her seat. Her breath smelled like vanilla ice cream. The crowd yelled "Espo seeeeeeeeto!", taunting the goalie, cheering for Tony.

Late in the third period, a Chicago player was checked

hard into the boards directly below Antonio's seat. The girl beside him covered her face. The game stopped and all the players skated slowly in circles, looking over toward Antonio. A man in a jogging suit and black shoes came running across the ice from the benches. Two other skaters lifted the injured player to his feet. He leaned on the boards and breathed heavily. Blood ran in lines down his face, and he spat red onto the ice. He was crying. He looked huge, much bigger than players ever looked on television or from the Greys. All the players suddenly looked huge. The girl's fingernails dug into his leg again.

"Is it over yet?" she asked.

The player turned and skated across the ice toward his bench. The crowd stood and applauded. On the glass just below Antonio, a wide streak of blood leaked downward in thin lines. Below it, on the ledge at the top of the boards, a tooth flashed white in a puddle of red. It looked to be dug into the wood. Antonio put his hand on top of the girl's fingers. She looked at him and touched his face.

"Are you okay, kiddo?" she said. Antonio nodded and threw up into her lap.

Tony's stewardship of the Cup began as he'd expected it to. Stan had always described with ironic amazement the disrespect and debauchery with which hockey players treated the thing they worked and sweated and lost teeth for. Sure, it was all kissing and smiling on the night of the big win, but after that, the Cup was just another possession in a long line of possessions. Stan taught Tony that very few players ever really understood the value of what they had won, and so Tony took over Stan's job with the same sense of protective disdain for all who treated the Cup poorly.

On the boardwalk in Atlantic City, New Jersey, with a crowd of press watching, a large seagull landed in the bowl of the Cup. It turned three quick circles, watching the people nearby and also looking out to sea, clicking its ringed yellow beak on the side of the bowl. There was laughter, and newspapers around the country picked up the wire photo, running it on the front page of their sports coverage. A determined, angry-looking bird nesting in the Cup. In the photo, there is an arm in dark suit material reaching for the bird, and the bird has pulled its head back behind its body, either trying to lean out of the way of the approaching arm or preparing to attack with its beak. The headline in *USA Today* ran, "New Jersey Resident Claims Cup as His Own." Tony wondered how they had determined the bird was a male. After that trip, he bought himself Audubon bird guides for all the regions he thought he might have to visit in his job.

When the bird landed, Tony was himself looking out to sea. Off the New Jersey coast, a cruise ship pushed north through moderate seas. Heading for New York, Tony thought and chuckled to himself. All that morning, Tony was reflecting on the newness of everything on this side of the continent. New Jersey, New England, even old New York was once New Amsterdam. The thought was moving around in his head, trying to incorporate a name like Virginia, but then the seagull had landed and Tony had moved on it.

Tony walked with a limp that entire day. The night before, a boy helping him bring the Cup through the lobby of the Trump Hotel had run into Tony's heel with the wheel of the dolly, opening the skin. Overnight, the wound had dried out and his ankle fused in a painful tightness. When he jumped forward to remove the bird, he felt the wound reopen.

Scott Marston, the Cup-winner from Atlantic City, threw up his breakfast ten minutes before the ceremony on the boardwalk. Behind a screen, Tony draped the Cup in its black velvet cover, noticing for the first time the number of birds that circled overhead. He wondered about bird feces. How one would remove them from black velvet. A scraper first, for sure, several passes with the light alcohol swab and then a good soft-brushing to straighten the grain. Marston had been with him for breakfast, and followed him onto the boardwalk, not wanting to see his family and friends until the ceremony. The morning sun and sea air had turned on him. Hungover from a night of rum and gambling with high school friends, Marston excused himself to one of the portable toilets beneath the boardwalk. As Tony made the final adjustments to the black velvet, he could hear Marston retching beneath him.

Tony watched the gull for a long time after it flew away. It had picked itself out of the Cup with a simple springing jump, like it had bounced. With its wings spread, the bird caught the perpetual ocean breeze and quickly drifted far beyond Tony's grasp. It dropped low over the sand and let loose a stream of white shit that just missed a young girl walking with her father. Over the water, it mingled with the other birds, but Tony kept it in sight despite the crowded skies. Two small grey and white feathers clung to the inside wall of the trophy's bowl. Tony pulled them away and heard a delicate static discharge like the distant ringing of tiny bells.

Ten

A t Aeroportul International Bucuresti Otopeni, Dragos Petrescu, his immediate family and Tony Chiello are photographed by two different young men, each with very expensive cameras. They are asked to pose formally, and no one will hear of Tony slipping out of the photograph. To the men with cameras, Tony is an important part of the story. They also take photos of the Cup but, strangely, do not ask Tony to remove it from the case. There are many young schoolgirls with armfuls of flowers. Tony is kissed and kissed again. He watches Petrescu receive his own flowers and speak with the red-faced girls, returning their kisses on both cheeks and slipping chocolate bars into their hands. The others too are receiving kisses and handing out little gifts. Tony wonders if it's possible they are all somehow related to each other. He is embarrassed to have nothing to give away.

Tony and the Cup are loaded into the rear seat of a bulky four-wheel drive. There is much shaking of hands and many new names. One of the photographers, a man in his twenties, climbs into the driver's seat and smiles back at Tony. Diana climbs into the back of the car as well, the bulky trophy case standing upright in the seat between them. Finally, Petrescu manages to pull himself from the crowd and climb into the front passenger seat. They leave the parking area at full speed, and Tony watches through the rear window as three Mercedes sedans pull out of the parking lot behind them. The driver introduces himself as Vasile.

"You also play hockey?" Vasile asks Tony.

"Where are we going?"

"Don't worry about where we're going. It is for me to wonder about where we are going. Are you on the same team?"

"I'm too short," Tony says, his eyes on the traffic speeding past them in the other direction. He is glad for the trophy case between him and Diana. He knows she's learning something about him, and does not want to see what effect it has on her face.

A cow grazes on the grassy avenue between lanes of a wide boulevard. An old man in a yellowing undershirt walks behind it with a long thin branch. He swats at the grass behind the cow's back hooves. Tony watches him for the few seconds it takes to pass in the car. The man's skin is burnt brown, and he whistles through toothless gums. Some kilometres past the cow, they stop at a light before a traffic circle. In the middle of the roadway, a fountain sends a wide spray into the air. Across the intersection, a man sits smoking on a stone bench. He wears a suit and tie and looks toward the car from behind dark sunglasses. He looks to be writing notes on a pad in his lap. The man raises his face toward the traffic circle, studies it for a moment and returns to his notepad. He has a high forehead, dented in the middle as though at a certain point in life he was struck by a hammer and somehow lived. Tony lowers his window. The air tastes of matches and thick exhaust. A mist from the fountain gathers around the car.

"You see these shoes?" Vasile asks, lifting his leg from below the steering wheel.

"Yes."

"These shoes belong to Ilie Năstase. He gave them to me."

Dragos laughs and says something in Romanian to Vasile, who also laughs. Diana does not laugh. Tony can see her hands resting calmly on her knees. He wonders if she has fallen asleep yet again.

"The tennis player?" Tony asks, not wanting to be left behind the language barrier so soon.

"Yes, you know another Ilie Năstase? I play at his club. He is a very generous man. We'll be passing very near his house. I'll show it to you."

"That's okay," Tony says. "I need to sleep."

"You will have much time to sleep in the grave." The light changes and Vasile starts forward, laughing. "Have you ever been to Ilie Năstase's house?"

"Of course not."

"Then, we go."

They pass a row of three horse-drawn carts. The carts ride on truck wheels and are driven by men in felt hats, women in brightly patterned dresses sitting beside them. Assorted children walk beside the carts or ride precariously between cargo.

"Gypsies," says Vasile. "They don't play tennis."

"Do they play hockey?" Tony asks.

This draws a sound from Diana, a soft snort of disgust,

and Tony knows she is paying attention to the conversation. Vasile shakes his head and waves a finger in the air.

"Yes, I know. I know. You are making a joke of me. I am capable of recognizing these jokes. My English is not so bad."

Tony changes the subject. "What is the name of the hotel?"

"Don't worry about the hotel. This is my country. You are my guest. You will be well taken care of."

Vasile turns from the boulevard onto a shaded, cobblestoned street. On the corner, two uniformed young men stand smoking. They lean in toward each other, stooped under the weight of the submachine rifles dangling from their shoulders. They look to be under twenty years old. They stare at Tony staring at them from the open window. Further down the street, a pack of dogs fight each other in the middle of the roadway. Vasile honks his horn and does not slow down. The dogs slip on either side of the car, still fighting, ignoring everything else.

"Năstase lives here?" Tony asks.

"Very near."

"This is the district of the embassies," Dragos says. "Very wealthy. Diana and I grew up not far from here, but of course, in a very different world."

"And the dogs?"

"What dogs?" Vasile growls.

They speed along the cobblestones. Streets open out into wide squares, sometimes centred on statues or monuments and sometimes not, always with one or two dogs sniffing at the periphery. They speed through the squares. The air is better, cooler, filtered by the canopy of leaves. Vasile pulls onto the sidewalk and stops in front of a wide wrought-iron gate.

"There he is. Năstase." Vasile waves madly from the driver's seat and honks his horn.

Through a darkly shaded entranceway behind the gate, Tony sees two men in white sitting at a patio table. Behind them is a glow of white on rust-red clay, canvas netting and crisply painted lines. A woman runs in and out of view at the centre of the glow, slamming hard at a tennis ball. The two men laugh and talk, taking turns throwing small dice onto the table. Vasile honks the horn again and steps from the car, his arms spread wide in front of him. The men leave their game and stroll to the gate, laughing and joking with Vasile. Tony can understand nothing. Neither man looks anything like the Ilie Năstase Tony remembers, but he can't be sure because he hasn't seen a photo of the famous tennis player in years.

He tries to picture either of these men accepting the trophy at Rolland Garos, lifting it over his head with that exhausted smile of the champion tennis player. He watches both men greet young Petrescu, the slapping of the back, the powerful shaking of hands. Through the locked gate, they kiss Diana on both cheeks, and for the first time Tony notices a blush in her face. He listens to the language for any recognizable sound. Then there is English.

"This is Antonio Chiello, from Canada—I told you."

One of the men steps forward and extends his arm toward the car window. Tony has not moved from his seat beside the trophy.

"Pleased to meet you. I'm Ilie."

Tony opens his door and slips from the back seat. He

leans across the sidewalk and shakes hands. The man is in late middle age, but slim and very muscular in that wiry way of the exceptional athlete.

"You play on the same team?" the man asks.

"I carry the trophy," Tony responds. It's the phrase Stan favoured in this situation. The situation that will always come up until, like Stan before him, Tony becomes obviously too old for it to be asked.

"You've brought it with you?"

"Yes. I go where it goes."

"Is that it in the car?"

"Yes. Would you like to see it?"

"Has Petrescu shown it to anyone else yet?"

"No. We've just arrived."

"Then I'll see it when he shows it. At the wedding. He won it?"

"Yes. His team."

"Do you play at all?" The man works at the lock on the gate with two fingers and indicates the inner courtyard with a flick of his jaw.

"Which? Hockey or tennis?"

The man laughs. His gate swings out into the sidewalk. "Backgammon. Do you play backgammon? I think you saw us playing here."

"I know how to play."

"But do you know how to win? Come, we'll play. Vasile, bring the car in here. It is safe."

Dragos and Tony climb back into the car and let Vasile drive them through the opened gate into the courtyard. Diana has already walked through the gate and made her way to the edge of the tennis court. The woman stops her tennis game when she sees Diana. She drops her racquet and screams, running to Diana to enfold her in a hug. Her opponent, another woman, walks toward them, patting at her face with a towel.

As they settle into their visit, a servant arrives with drinks for everyone—small tumblers of vodka, and a full bottle beside them on the tray. Seeing there is a game in progress, the servant avoids the table and gently places the tray on an unused chair. He then picks up one of the tumblers for himself and downs the contents in a single gulp. The patio table is decorated in a backgammon mosaic. The pieces are of polished stone and the dice are far heavier than they looked, as though made of lead. The man who calls himself Ilie Năstase sits opposite Tony, rubbing the dice between his hands before each throw.

"Tennis? Please. It's very nice," he says. "It has done nice things for me, as you can see. And hockey, yes, also very exciting, very athletic. But backgammon, this is our national sport. This is the pride of my country. Would I trade my professional trophies for a chance to play for Romania at the table? Maybe not—no certainly not. But I would trade almost anything else. Am I right, Mr. Petrescu?"

Dragos smiles, but his expression is unconvincing, even to Tony. "For you perhaps. You have a great deal to trade."

The game proceeds with embarrassing rapidity, Tony feeling from his very first roll that he has seated himself at a game he only thought he understood. The man named Ilie completes his final roll, taking the game.

"You see, to be great at tennis is an honourable, excellent thing in Romania. But to be truly great at backgammon… that *is* Romania."

Tony stares at the table, his pieces scattered haphazardly across it, two of them still stranded ridiculously on the bar.

"Perhaps I should play you at tennis," Tony says to his smiling opponent. "to make myself feel better."

Diana begins resetting the board. She looks Tony in the eyes, and Tony sees anger touch down briefly on the young woman's face. Early in the visit, Diana had excused herself to the bathroom. Whatever she had done there makes her look suddenly glamorous, erasing the fatigue of long travel. Her hair is now perfectly brushed and arranged, falling across her eyes as she sets the pieces. As she leans across the table, her shirt front opens to Tony and he glimpses there a black bra strap against the whitest of skin.

"Perhaps this time, you should try," Diana says.

Ilie and the young hockey player laugh into their empty vodka glasses. Vasile and the other guest have fallen asleep in their chairs, victimized by drink. The servant is busily filling a new tray of glasses. The other women laugh and drift back to the tennis court. Diana finishes with the board and slaps the dice in front of Ilie. She stands behind Tony, and a new game begins.

Eleven

Tony, the Cup, the young champion and his beautiful cousin fly the final leg of their journey aboard a rattling turboprop on Tarom, the Romanian national airline. Somehow, in the transfer through Bucharest, Dragos's father and aunt have left the travelling party. Tony's mind has begun to shut in on itself in a whirl of new information. He fidgets with the locks on the trophy case, finding solace in repetition.

Taxiing before takeoff, the plane passes by several of its own kind abandoned in rusted hulks behind a chain fence on the side of the runway. The ever-present Romanian dogs have made homes of these shells. They stick their heads from the empty doorways, sniffing the air and peering suspiciously at Tony's plane as it passes on the tarmac. Tony tries not to wonder how the doghouse planes have ended up there, their propellers bent, their wheel rims shorn of all rubber. The plane takes to the air at sunset and makes the trip in three dark hours of turbulence and engine-howl.

Sitting, as usual, across the aisle from Tony, Dragos struggles to keep up a conversation. The closer he draws to his old life, the more agitated and talkative he becomes. Earlier, at Năstase's house in the heart of privileged Bucharest, it had not been hard for Tony to see Dragos as a man comfortably at home, laughing and joking in his native language. Now he wonders if that sense of belonging had been just a matter of Dragos being in the presence of another elite athlete. Here, suspended above the Romanian countryside, flying into the heart of a Romanian night on his way to marriage in an ancient Romanian ceremony, the young man struggles to hide his fear.

Fear of what, Tony can't imagine. To return to your family the celebrated hero of a Cup-winning team? This has been, for Tony, the only truly comfortable fantasy for too long. How could such a golden reality generate anything but blissful satisfaction?

"Your problem with the game, Tony, is that you play to win."

Tony blinks at the younger man, confused.

"You must play to destroy. Trying to pick your way home safely all the time, that is well for beginners in the game, but a champion must know when to take chances, when to have courage."

"Ah, backgammon," Tony nods. "Yes, courage, that's fine, but he had the better dice every time."

"Who, Năstase? Please, Tony, if that man played tennis the way he trips around the backgammon board, he would still be retrieving balls for the rich at some spa in Constanța. Năstase's dice were no better than your dice. The difference was he was able to take the drive to destroy that he uses in tennis and use it as well on the board. Năstase decided to beat you; that's why he beat you."

"Well, I think I tried to destroy him."

"No, Tony, you tried to not lose. You played like the hockey team that goes up 3-nil in the first period and then slowly lets it all slide into the toilet."

Diana joins in, not hiding the disgust in her voice.

"I know it is not polite in the man's own home," she says, "but, Tony, you should have tried to humiliate him. A game is for winning. It's nothing personal; everyone knows that, everyone here anyway."

"The country of champions. Romania!"

"Yes, that's funny." Diana speaks to him, but her face is turned toward her own window. In effect, Tony is being spoken to by the reflection of Diana's face in the Romanian night.

"You say funny things about this country. I wish I could think of something funny to say about Canada for you."

"No, Romania is not a country of champions, you are right." Dragos puts himself between them again. "But it is a country that knows every game, no matter how friendly, no matter how sociable, holds within it a grain of the ultimate struggle. You should tell me now what is more important than the ultimate struggle."

"Okay, the ultimate struggle," Tony says wearily. "I was engaged in the ultimate struggle with a retired tennis champion, if that's even who he was. I lost at backgammon to someone who may or may not be Ilie Năstase. And yet, I don't feel any great sense of loss."

Tony wonders how the loss of a casual match as a guest in someone's house has turned him into Diana's enemy. Since leaving Năstase's compound after a 3-1 embarrassment, the young woman has steadfastly refused to even look in Tony's direction.

"Really, Tony?" Diana continues to address the window. "Where I grew up in Bucharest, the three streets we considered our neighbourhood, this game was a way of life. At every street corner you would see two or more old men sitting around tables or benches, either playing or watching someone else play. You know, a great many of the old neighbourhoods there in central Bucharest were taken away by Ceauşescu, the houses nationalized and then brought to the ground to make way for the new wide avenues surrounding that idiocy he called his palace. Yet even after the houses disappeared, the same old men would show up at the same street corners and play the same games again and again."

Diana is now not talking to anyone—she is simply talking, and Tony begins to suspect this mood that has overcome both these young Romanians has very little to do with him. The country has done this to them. Something they left behind when they escaped from Romania years before has found them again, and overtaken them. Some disappointment. Some anger.

"You would not find one of those men who would say as you do that to lose a game means not to lose anything important. They could be forced from their homes and into any one of the hundreds of identically ugly apartments that were built back then, but they could not be forced from their game. Our grandfather has played a match of fifteen games every day with the same man for almost forty years now. It is the doctor, Fischoff, the same man who delivered both of our fathers and both of us. For forty years this man has delivered babies and removed tumours and watched old people die, and for the same forty years he has taken time in each day to meet my grandfather in the park near the hospital for a match of fifteen games."

"I see," Tony says, working to keep all sarcasm from his tone. "That's some important game then. I'm sorry. I didn't realize."

Diana suddenly climbs from her seat, slips across the lap of her cousin and lands in stockinged feet in the aisle beside Tony. She leans down and kisses him on the mouth, using a skinny hand behind his head to pull him hard against her lips.

"I thought so," she says, and climbs back over her cousin.

Tony says nothing. He sits and pays attention to the burning of his lips and the memory of Diana's fingernails digging into the back of his head. The lights in the airplane blink out for several seconds as they hit a particularly bad patch of air. In the darkness, Tony concentrates on the sound of the seat belt straining against the black carrying case beside him. Diana starts talking again, her voice shaking with the vibrations of the flight. Again, Tony relaxes, resigned to listen.

In the late 1970s, a woman named Vera lived in one of the square, dull concrete apartment blocks built on a new street full of square dull concrete apartment blocks near the Victory Plaza in Bucharest. Vera's street, Titulescu Avenue, was named for a public servant who won small fame for having resisted the Fascist push of the mid-'30s. A statue of an uninteresting businesslike figure still stands at the head of her street, where the streetcars turn from Victory Boulevard. Vera was in her late fifties, but a grandmother of some years. Her granddaughter Andrea lived with her in a one-bedroom apartment on the second floor that was also home to Vera's husband Serban and Serban's invalid mother. What had become of Andrea's parents, no one knew.

"I was in junior school with Andrea," Diana says. "She was older by some years, and used to take care of the younger children after school until we were picked up. There were girls more beautiful, but she had all the talent."

Serban was a tour guide for the Ministry of Culture and was more often than not out of Bucharest leading tours through the medieval monasteries near the northern border with the Soviet Union. The responsibility for Andrea's education fell to Vera, and it worried her greatly. Andrea was coming to the age when she would have to leave elementary school and take her place in one of the focused higher schools. Bucharest academies were filled with children of the governmental elite. Acceptance in the better academies depended much more on connection than merit, but exceptions were made when the state recognized a talent worth supporting. In both sport and art, talent still helped to determine advancement, not always, but often. Vera knew her granddaughter was such a talent. She knew Andrea could play violin in the National Orchestra. For a year, she had investigated procedures for admittance to the best music academies in the city. For a year, she had sent official letters to boards of admittance, and received no reply. She became aware the official silence was a reaction to the return address on her envelopes.

Titulescu Avenue was two streets beyond the inner circle of power and privilege in Bucharest. Vera lived near enough to power to shop at the same market with the servants of government wives, but, in correspondence, she wore her address like a disfiguring scar. Power and privilege lived on the tree-lined streets named for the greater cosmopolitan: Strada Paris, Strada Sofia, or grand avenues named for the great and happy Communist flowering, Victory Boulevard, Avenue of the First of May. To live on a street named for a bureaucrat, no matter his prominence, was to have one's potential defined. In six months, Andrea would have to have a place in an academy. Vera saw her granddaughter's future slipping into mediocrity. Some strategy other than letters would have to be employed.

"Our entire family," Dragos interrupts his cousin, "lived on Kisselef. A much better address. The neighbourhoods were like separate cities."

Through talks with the servants at the First of May Market, Vera heard stories of how women of privilege secured spots at the conservatory for their daughters, whether these girls showed musical promise or not. The conservatory was an academy greatly desired among privileged mothers of privileged daughters. Young government men prided themselves on public displays of cultural knowledge. Four times a year the recital hall was filled with young, unmarried men at the outset of brilliant careers. These men would drink cognac together in the foyer and speak about important government matters. Then they would sit and watch the beautiful daughters of their superiors send music into the night. It was unheard of for a recital to pass without at least five proposals of marriage exchanged between young men in dark suits and tittering girls carrying instruments. As often as not, these girls played only passable music, their talent being employed exclusively with the aim of securing a privileged married life. Often their mothers encouraged this scheme because they themselves had been successful at it earlier in life.

A population of music tutors existed within the inner circles of the powerful. These tutors, mostly men of middle age, worked with the privileged daughters in the year leading up to admissions trials. Whether blessed with natural talent or not, these young girls were imparted enough skills with an instrument to give a reasonable trial recital that, combined with their home address and some well-placed gifts of cognac and fine imported cheeses, assured them both a place at the conservatory and a potential young fiancé in a dark suit.

All tutors were courted furiously, the struggle for their favour and influence was desperately competitive. The most sought after tutors provided not just music lessons, but a solid guarantee of success built of their long-standing connections with the members of the conservatory admissions board. A student who arrived for recital on the arm of one of these influential men never failed to secure a place for herself. Handing over the last available Sibiu salami to a smiling maidservant, Vera obtained the name and address of one of the most popular tutors in Bucharest. She wrote it on the bottom of her shopping list and returned the sweaty paper to her brassiere.

Valentin Popescu was a large man who would sweat in mid-winter after walking only a block. In every season, he carried with him a collection of handkerchiefs, which he used to wipe his forehead and neck. Handkerchiefs were primary among the favoured gifts he received from the mothers of his students. He carried with him at all times a collection of French centimes which he used to "pay" for these unusual presents, handkerchiefs being symbols of grief and permanent separation and therefore much out of favour as tokens of affection.

"You remember him?" Diana asks her cousin. "He was like a pig on two legs. Disgusting." Dragos laughs and snorts. The cabin lights flicker again, like the opening strip of film running through a bad projector. Tony wonders about electrical shorts in wires behind the walls.

Eyeing a particularly fine piece of linen or silk, Popescu would reach two fingers into his pocket and produce a single, well-polished centime with which he would offer to buy the cloth. Thus charmed out of their instinctual superstition, the mothers of his students would gladly accept the beautiful foreign coin and hand over the cloth that would next serve to remove perspiration from Popescu's beaded brow. As a consequence of his talent with violin instruction and his eminent connections with the admissions board, Valentin Popescu had a collection of handkerchiefs from the finest clothiers in Europe. When wiping his forehead while in conversation with one of his peers at the conservatory, he did not fail to stop and gaze at the moist cloth, and to proudly drop the name of the woman who had given it to him.

"This lovely kerchief I purchased from the widow Popovici for a single centime. Her daughter is to be married to the junior secretary of the Typographers Union. The cloth belonged, she said, to her dearly departed husband who purchased it in Strasbourg while on a research tour. He was very prominent in the Department of Agriculture, you know. His arena was cheese, I believe."

Professor Popescu, as he preferred to be addressed, was also a great admirer of cheese. The woman who obtained his services for her daughter would invariably spend the next eight months bargaining with market owners for the finest selection of cheeses in the capital. A joke went about the conservatory that for each wheel of Camembert that entered the city in some diplomat's briefcase, a full one-fifth went into Professor Popescu's stomach.

Vera learned these details at the First of May Market. For a week, she gave up her place in line, took inferior cuts of meat and shared her produce with these servant women in order to hear their stories of the great professor. She needed to know all she could before approaching him. She knew his response to her address would be the same as the conservatory's, and she needed an advantage. The handkerchiefs and the cheese would help, but she was unsure how she would compete with the connected wives of diplomats in these gifts. One day, she was stopped on the street outside the market by a woman name Mariana Mururescu, a cook for the well-placed family Ganea.

"My dear lady," Mariana said to Vera, "the answer to your problem is backgammon."

The wife of Stefan Ganea, deputy to the director of foreign affairs, had recently secured the help of Professor Popescu for her daughter Lutzi. Mariana Mururescu had observed Vera's struggles at the market, overheard her questions about the great Professor and so kept her eyes open for advantage. On that very morning, Mariana had happened to pass through the side door of the house, rather than the back door on her way to the market. The side door led to the carport where the Ganeas' government chauffeur spent his days. Responsible only for taking Ganea to work and returning him home, with the occasional out-of-town government function to attend, the chauffeur spent most days polishing the official black Mercedes sedan and the smaller, but no less black, Dacia, cleaning from them the muck and filth and dog shit of Bucharest.

As Mariana stepped from the side door into the carport that morning, there was Popescu, seated on an overturned wooden bucket and crouched over a game of backgammon. Ganea's chauffeur sat across from him on the third rung of a small stepladder. Neither man looked up when she entered. They were involved in a furious endgame, mesmerized by the dancing of the dice as they raced to clear their houses. Mariana stopped and watched the conclusion. Popescu won, clearing all his pieces from the board one roll ahead of the chauffeur. He laughed with happy relief at the final roll and immediately wiped his entire face with a startlingly blue cotton handkerchief. The chauffeur began resetting the board for the next game.

"Lucky this time," he said.

"It's my day," returned Popescu, "I feel it."

"You'll need more than one good day," laughed the younger man. "The account is heavy in my favour."

"It will turn," said Popescu. "It will turn. I feel it."

Only then did the tutor look up from the game to see Mariana standing some four feet away, watching with amused interest. He rose from the wooden bucket as quickly as his weight would allow and stood fumbling to return his handkerchief to his inside jacket pocket.

"Ah, my dear Mariana," he began, "you must be a friend to me and not mention this game to your employers. You know how it is with us servants. We must hang together."

"Professor, you lower yourself unnecessarily," Mariana laughed. "Surely a man of your standing can choose when and how he amuses himself. And please sir, I do not tell tales on others. It pleases me to see you here, that's all. To see you enjoying yourself so. Such passion."

"Yes, passion, I'm afraid with me, kind woman, it is more of an obsessive love than a fleeting passion. But you are a woman of honour, comrade. I thank you for your discretion. Consider me in your debt."

Mariana recounted to Vera other times when the professor's curious obsession had revealed itself, how she had thought nothing of it but how he had struggled to conceal it from the family Ganea. Chess, not backgammon, is the game of the intelligent member of Bucharest's elite, a game of intellect and cunning. Backgammon's dependence on dice and chance to decide its outcome lowers it in the eyes of the powerful. As well, chess showed one's connection to high Russian culture while backgammon told of Romania's long and antagonistic relationship with the devil Turks. Chess was played in parlours, offices and sitting rooms, while one could find backgammon being contested on street corners and the third-class sections of overnight trains.

"He is embarrassed to be seen by important people playing this game," Mariana explained. "It is very well for him to sit and eat and discuss music and gossip with Ganea, but when he wants to play his game, he must sneak around and sit on buckets."

"Is he good?"

"An amateur. He was lucky to win when he did. I saw three mistakes when he was bearing off alone. If you are good yourself, you will have to be careful how you let him win."

Mariana left Vera contemplating her new understanding of the professor Valentin Popescu. Before turning in that night she had completed a new handkerchief for the powerful tutor. Strips of red and gold coloured cloth expertly sewn to a field of white linen creating a perfect miniature backgammon board. In one corner she embroidered the standard VP, and in the other a pair of dice showing 6 and 5, her own favourite opening roll.

Two weeks later, Valentin Popescu showed displeasure on his face, and in his impatience to leave. He had been in the little apartment less than five minutes before he began looking at his pocket watch and making protestations about his schedule. Vera barely had time to make coffee before he was pacing the living room floor, working up his excuse for a hasty exit. It didn't help his mood that he had not stopped sweating from the exertion of climbing two flights of stairs. He had never tutored a girl who did not live in a house. He was worried about walking on Titulescu Avenue after dark. He had seen many Gypsies on his way in, and the train station was so close he could hear the cries of beggar children from the sidewalk outside Vera's building.

Vera worked at the coffee in the kitchen, listening anxiously to make sure the tutor did not slip back outside. If he left before she could speak with him, she would surely never see him again. She read that certainty in his eyes as he came through the door, and she could hear it amplified in the grunts of displeasure that reached her from the living room.

The apartment's one main room barely contained him.

His large frame bumped against the dining table, and he found it difficult to squeeze past the chairs set in a semicircle in front of the television. Wanting to moisten his handkerchief and wipe his face, Popescu began opening doors. There were only two options, but his luck was bad and the door he tried opened to reveal a bedroom in semi-darkness. The bed was perfectly made and framed at the head and feet by wooden bookshelves overflowing with magazines. He stepped inside and examined the shelves. Every magazine contained nothing but crossword puzzles and, picking one or two up, it seemed to Popescu that every single puzzle had been completed. Then, a voice.

"Have you come with soup?"

The question came from the darkest corner of the room, and it electrified him to the spot. Sweat had begun to cool on his forehead, but now it flowed again, hot and fresh. An impossibly old woman sat in a padded chair, almost obliterated by shadow but with a magazine and pencil in her hand. She was not looking at Popescu, but rather she worked with studied concentration on a crossword. She was dressed as though to go to the theatre, but her shoes were removed and placed beside the chair. Instead, she wore large red slippers, men's slippers in fact, that appeared many sizes too large for her tiny feet. Popescu could think of no answer to her question. Instead, he stood and stared, terrified of her oldness and wishing he had not ventured onto Titulescu Avenue. Hearing no reply, the woman raised her eyes from her puzzle.

"Ah, Monsieur, it is a pleasure. Have we met?"

"We have not, Madame."

The tutor was surprised to hear perfect French from such

a creature in such a place.

"You have the look of a boy I knew once. He was a musician. He loved me desperately, but I was of course already married at the time. A friend of my son."

"An unfortunate man."

"Yes, well of course I gave myself to him, but he wanted more. Eventually he stepped beneath a train."

"It's tragic."

He looked more closely, and there was indeed a charming face beneath her age. He tried to recall stories of young musicians leaping onto train tracks.

"And you have no soup for me?"

"No Madame, I have come at the request of your daughter, Vera. I am a professor at the conservatory. She wished to speak with me on some matter."

"Yes, yes, I know it."

The woman pulled herself very slowly forward on the chair. Popescu crossed the room in two steps and bent to lend his arm. The old woman leaned lightly on his elbow and gently levered herself across to the bed.

"I am 94 years old. I had my first lover in the last century and my last lover at the midpoint of this century. Now my son's wife brings me soup and helps me use the bathroom. If I could, maybe I also would step beneath a train."

"You are still very beautiful, Madame."

"Yes, I am. Of course."

Vera came to the door and, her hand on a sweaty elbow, pulled the tutor back into the living room. Then she carried a tray with soup and coffee into the bedroom and placed it on top of the bookshelf closest to the bed. On her way back out, she shut the door.

"She will sleep after she eats. I am sorry if she disturbed you. Sometimes she forgets where she is."

On the dining table Vera had laid out a coffee tray with fresh bread and a small assortment of goat and sheep cheeses. Behind the table, on the wall, hung a handmade backgammon board. Vera's husband Serban had made it for himself out of scrap wood and the cedar wrappings of Cuban cigars. While guiding Cuban diplomats around the northern monasteries, Serban had collected the wrappings one by one when they dropped to the floor after dinner. Back in Bucharest, he had sliced twenty-four of them into backgammon spikes and glued them to a board. The effect was completed with stains and finishes he borrowed from a local artisan. He then hand-carved each of the pieces and the two dice from a willow branch. Popescu stared at the board as he ate his meal. Vera smiled at him.

They played each evening for two hours. Vera let him win many games, but not all of them, and she gradually raised the level of her game so that his wins took more out of him. The challenge was intoxicating to both of them. He listened to Andrea play her violin, but only incidentally as she practised on the balcony or in her great-grandmother's bedroom. The lure of the game was so powerful that Vera felt no need to dissemble her motives. She told the tutor on the first evening that she wanted his help to get Andrea into the conservatory. She told him this and then she beat him ruthlessly in a quick game. He accepted the job, and she beat him a second straight time. Then she eased up a bit and let him scrape out his share of wins. The first night ended in a tie. Before he left, she presented him with the red and gold backgammon handkerchief. Popescu could not contain his

delight with the object and he immediately dug a shiny centime from his pocket to pay for it. Andrea was sent to walk
him back to the embassy district. There were two months
remaining until the next admissions audition.

The money Vera had hidden away in her cushions
disappeared. Each new week meant fresh cheeses from the
countryside and a new handkerchief to create. Popescu
would assign Andrea several pieces to learn over the
course of each week and on Thursday evenings she would
present a small concert in the living room while her
grandmother and the tutor wrestled with the dice on the
handmade wooden board. Serban returned from the north
for two weeks. Popescu made him nervous, and when he
was nervous he liked to drink țuică. And so, together, Vera
and Serban discovered another of the great tutor's passions.
Serban had arrived back in Bucharest with four bottles of
the homemade plum brandy, gifts from farmers with whom
he'd billeted tourists. He returned to the north with four
empty bottles.

Unfortunately, when he drank, Popescu became lazy at
the game, and Vera was forced to work harder and be trick-
ier in her concessions. With her husband home, Vera could
not help but win much more than she lost. Strangely, it only
made Popescu more determined to continue the tournament. Vera happily let her cushion money turn to cheese
and disappear down the tutor's throat. When she saw Mariana in the morning, the two women laughed and squeezed
each other's hands for luck. Each night, Vera worked the
board in intense concentration. Each night, Popescu felt
he was on the verge of a breakthrough victory. Each night,
Andrea practised or played, and then walked her tutor safely

JOHN DEGEN

through the empty streets.

A little more than one week from the audition, Vera awoke in the darkness of morning to the sound of her grand-daughter crying. Normally, Andrea slept with her on the daybed in the living room, the two of them pressed together for warmth. Andrea's sobs were quiet, muted because they came from the old woman's bedroom. It was a sound Vera had long expected to hear from that room, and they woke her immediately.

"How will I tell Serban?" she wondered.

But when she opened the bedroom door, Andrea lay on the bed, and her great-grandmother, far from dead, sat beside her, rubbing a hand between her shoulder blades.

"It is the oldest story," the old woman said, not bothering to look up at her daughter-in-law.

"He loves her, but she doesn't love him. But he is the man, so she loves him anyway. The oldest of stories. I've lived it many times myself."

Vera wept on Mariana's shoulders outside the market. After she heard the little that Andrea had told Vera, Mariana used her extensive servant's network to check the story. It was true. The great tutor loved handkerchiefs, and cheese. He had a passion for liquor and an obsession with an ancient game. But above all he loved his students. Popescu had slept with almost every young girl he helped into the conservatory, even the homely Lutzi Ganea. For the most part, the girls' parents remained unaware of the affair, but in several instances mothers willingly whored their daughters to the influential professor for the prospect of a spot in the academy and a good marriage.

The trysts had begun on the tutor's walks back from Vera's

apartment. Andrea walked beside him, her arm through his, as was the custom when men and women walked together on the street. When he kissed her the first time, she had wanted to run, but was terrified of destroying all her grandmother's hard work on her behalf. Over the weeks the kisses turned more passionate. Once he managed to talk Andrea into the park on the edge of Kisselef Boulevard. There, in the shadow of Stalin's great stone statue, the fat tutor had reached beneath her blouse and squeezed her breasts. He slipped a hand under her skirt and struggled with her underwear, and would certainly have raped her, but he was frightened by the voices of a Gypsy family clopping along the boulevard on their horse-drawn cart.

Convinced Popescu would abandon her at the audition if she didn't cooperate, Andrea let the affair continue. Every night her grandmother would work hard to disguise her overwhelming superiority at backgammon and every night Andrea would work to hide her disgust and fear. She kissed the professor willingly at the end of their walks, and even pretended to enjoy it, but made excuses for not going into the park. He made her promise she would find time for them to be alone indoors. She managed for a while to put obstacles in the way of such a meeting, but was running out of time and excuses. If she did not sleep with him before the audition, it was certain she would not be accepted, and her grandmother would die from disappointment. It was at this point that Andrea lay awake all night worrying and finally collapsed into tears on her great-grandmother's bed. The old woman's affairs were family legends, but her advice to Andrea had been too cruel for her to imagine.

"If accepting his penis gets you what you need, then accept

his penis. There are worse things than a penis. Though he is not the best looking young man I've ever seen."

Vera excused herself from meeting with Popescu for two nights. On both nights, she and her granddaughter sat together in the living room and talked. Andrea played for her the pieces that she was practising for the audition. Her music was perfect, but they both knew, without the tutor's help, it would not make a difference how well she played. For the first time, Vera told stories about her time in prison. She showed Andrea letters and newspaper clippings she had kept hidden away in the backs of cupboards for thirty years.

When Popescu was admitted back into Vera's apartment, there were four days remaining until the audition. Vera brought him some dinner at the table and sat down opposite him. Andrea listened from the bedroom.

"It is only right that you have my granddaughter," she began.

Popescu swallowed slowly and placed his cutlery on the tabletop.

"I don't like it," Vera continued. "She is just a young girl and you must know she is not in love with you."

"Madame, you mistake me."

He made a small gesture of protest, but felt little need to be convincing. He'd been in similar situations before. He usually held all the power, and even more so on Titulescu Avenue.

"As I said, I don't like it. But, like you, I am aware of your rights in this situation. How does one put a price on a good start in life? Me, I've worked since Andrea was born, since before she was born, to help her get a good start in life. I have saved many, many dollars, American dollars, to make this happen. But you set the price, and that is your right."

The tutor resumed his meal with a smile.

"That is my right," he said. "I have also worked very hard, and I deserve my compensations. There has never been a complaint, not even from newlywed husbands. My price is reasonable for what is offered."

"It is reasonable, I agree. But I won't pay it. I have talked with Andrea for two nights. We have talked it in both directions. We have looked at all the details of this situation. She is willing to pay the price, but I am not willing to have her pay it. If it were her decision, you would have your way tonight, in this very apartment, but a grandmother has one right in the end, and that is the right of final decision in matters like this."

"You should think some more about this," Popescu said, playing his advantage. "The audition is so close, and a space will be made. She has so much talent, it will be a simple case and will seem perfectly correct."

"I will not pay it," Vera insisted. "I've said that, and you cannot make me change my mind."

Popescu wiped his mouth and pushed himself back in his chair. His face remained dry and without shame.

"The cheese was not very good these last nights," he said, and stood to leave.

"I won't pay it, but I will risk it."

Vera pulled the board from the wall and placed it in the traditional spot on the table. She cleared away the dinner dishes and brought a bottle of vodka from the kitchen. Popescu had reseated himself and was grinning at the board, his eyes gleaming. Never before had he played for such delicious stakes.

"It is an excellent decision," he said, rubbing the dice together between sweaty hands.

"Seven matches, five games each match. If you win the tournament, you may do what you wish with my granddaughter. And it is up to you whether she is admitted to the conservatory. As well, I will provide a meal for you three times a week for the rest of my life."

"Excellent decision," the tutor bowed to Vera. "You are a woman of honour."

"But if you do not win the tournament, you must pay my price. You must admit Andrea to the conservatory and see to it she graduates from the program. You must not touch her again, and this family is released from all claims."

"Madame, if you win this tournament, I will do all those things, and more. I will make sure she is given a place on the travelling orchestra. If you win, Madame, your precious Andrea will play in Paris and in Rome. Your granddaughter will play in Moscow, Madame. If you win, Madame."

Vera opened the door to the bedroom and helped Andrea carry her great-grandmother onto the daybed in the living room. Andrea sat beside the old woman and held her steady against a mound of cushions. She looked directly into the tutor's eyes and smiled sweetly.

"You must make your promise in front of us all, Professor Popescu. This is a match of honour, and it must be witnessed. My mother-in-law will hear your terms."

Popescu repeated his pledge to the old woman, and also, gleefully, explained in detail the prize he would win for defeating Vera.

"It is fair," the old woman said. "I will die very soon, most likely within this year. You have made a pledge to the dying, sir. Are you sure you want to take this risk, because you must honour it?"

"It is the greatest gamble I've ever been offered. I must play."

As he walked home along Titulescu Avenue alone, his limbs shaking and his skin slick with perspiration, Valentin Popescu could not help himself from crying. He cried for his lost Andrea, for the sweetness of her virginity. He wept because she was the first young girl he had decided to have, whom he would in fact never have. Mostly he cried at the recollection of his play during the tournament, at the understanding he now had of his clumsiness, his ineptitude, his drought of expertise. His eyes filled with tears of shame for himself, and admiration for this old woman, this Vera, who played the board as though it were not a question of dice.

Each year following, until her death, on the anniversary of Andrea's triumphant audition recital, Vera made a pilgrimage to the conservatory in the centre of the city. If Andrea was in the country, she would accompany her grandmother, but when the young violinist was travelling with her orchestra Vera would go alone. And each year she would tie onto the iron gates of the school a newly sewn handkerchief, in the design of a backgammon board.

"Andrea still plays for the National Orchestra," Diana says, staring through the window at the impenetrable night. "I saw her once in New York. She is quite famous."

The small plane lands late in the evening in the city of Suceava, near the northeastern border with Moldova. At the airport there, Tony and Diana are separated from

Dragos who is dragged from the gate by old friends anxious to give the groom one last night of debauchery. They ride with the Cup the final forty kilometres to the village of Ilisesti in the rear seat of a black Mercedes sedan, a uniformed driver silent in the front. Again Tony and Diana are kept apart in the back seat by the large black travelling case, which is just as well, since Tony can think of nothing to say in response to her kiss and the story of Vera. Leaving Suceava, Tony lowers his window. Where Bucharest's air had been hot and choking with smog, here the night smells of pine forest and long fragrant grasses. Tony slips down in the soft leather upholstery, pressing his knees against the front passenger seat. As they drive, he can hear Diana breathing slowly and heavily, and with nothing to see out the windows, he glides off into sleep.

Twelve

Tony's grandfather killed animals in the family garage, one block south of Danforth Avenue in Toronto throughout the year, following a strict calendar of blood. It was illegal to slaughter one's own meat in the city, but if the old man understood the law, he didn't care about it. He killed animals for himself, for his family and for many of the neighbours. In the spring it was a lamb for Easter, during the summer, goats and chickens. Never a pig, though he threatened to kill one, a young one, every year. In the winter months, and whenever there was time, he caught pigeons and songbirds, ringing their necks on his way through the alleyway and plucking them at his chair beside the woodstove in the garage. If he didn't cook the birds in a stew that day, he put them in individual plastic baggies and froze them. The freezer in the basement of Tony's childhood home was filled with the carcasses of pigeons and songbirds.

Tony avoided the garage and the smell of blood, though he often could not because the garage was the only place to find his grandfather when he wasn't in the house. Sent to fetch the old man for dinner, Tony would stand outside the killing zone, by the raspberry bushes, calling into the warm gloom. He would pick handfuls of raspberries and crush them into his mouth to smother the smell of guts and blood. His grandfather always seemed hard of hearing when Tony came to get him, yet the old man was able to hear a starling near the feeder in the front yard from his seat by the wood-stove. Tony tried not to look at the things in the garage, and the old man tried to make him look. The lamb was always the worst. Hanging from the chain on a wooden crossbeam in the roof, the Easter lamb looked too young for death. Its body deflated, unusable, and Tony wondered where it was they scraped the delicious meat from. The lamb dripped into a galvanized steel bucket, eyes open, surprised by the knife. The tongue always curled out between the teeth. The head went for soup.

At that age, two years before the onset of adolescence, had they cared to notice him in this way, Tony might have been a philosophical liability to his family. He was a tender thinker, and to live comfortably in his family, that was a bad way to be. If not bad, then unhelpful and certainly unpro-ductive. The tender thoughts might have been helpful for the lamb or the birds if Tony was in any position to act on them, but he wasn't. The slaughter of animals continued despite Tony's opinions and feelings. The family went on eating the meat of songbirds. The neighbours visited the garage to receive their share.

Killing thrived in the neighbourhood. If they didn't actu-ally need to live in this way, they at least thought they did, and so it was a lifestyle that justified itself. The existence of an overstocked produce department in the supermarket just blocks away did not stop any of the families in Tony's neighbourhood from growing their own vegetables. Yards resembled farms, and the rhythm of growing set the clocks. To break the tiny neck bones of birds was to admit that the sun had moved through the sky again.

Finding a wounded pigeon in the alleyway one evening, Tony hid it from his grandfather. He confined it under a cardboard box beneath the porch for a day until he could manage to move it higher. He built a three-sided perch for the bird from discarded wooden shingles, and lay terrified and red-faced on the slant of the roof to hammer the structure safely under the eaves. One wing refused to fold properly, but otherwise the bird seemed strong. With rest and food, Tony reasoned, it would mend itself and fly away from the danger of his neighbourhood. Every morning, while his grandfather toured the gardens and garages of the street, Tony snuck into the alley to feed his pigeon. He nailed the lid of a sauce jar to the end of a pole, and used wire to secure that pole to another pole. The two poles together reached the perch under the shadow of the eaves, and in this way Tony managed to pour a handful of cracked corn into the bird every morning. He stole the cracked corn from a bag just inside the garage. It was normally used for bait. There were hand-sized piles of cracked corn tempting birds to every corner of the yard and garden.

This was the lesson Tony learned from his wounded pigeon, a lesson in leaving things be. Had he left the bird fluttering and unable to fold its one wing, had he followed one of his immediate impulses and walked away from it, the bird would have managed one of two things. It would have somehow made its own way out of danger, walking or somehow hopping itself into a safe place, healing its wing over time and then escaping. Or it might have died much more quickly. A fluttering, injured bird in that alleyway would most likely finish in the jaws of a cat or the hands of an old man, both quick if not painless ways out of the world. Tony's bird lived several days longer. It watched a few sunrises over the eastern roofs of the neighbourhood, ate some cracked corn, and then died anyway, the victim of a young boy's tender thinking and its own growing strength.

On its fourth afternoon in the shingle perch, the pigeon began to stretch and test its injured wing. It unfolded and flapped and managed to make things right, and in doing all that, it made a lot of noise under the eaves and sent a lot of cracked corn falling to the cement below. While Tony learned something at school, and while the bird tested and retested its healing wing, Tony's grandfather took a pole wired to another pole, removed a jar lid that had been attached to the end, and drove several long nails through so they protruded like the spikes on a cruel medieval weapon. It was a wonderful tool and Tony's grandfather was proud that he'd invented it. The bird died easily on the first or second strike and stuck to the spikes for easy retrieval. Tony's pigeon was the first of many unfortunates to use that shingle perch. The old man built five more like it, and turned the alley eaves into a pigeon farm, fattening the birds that landed there with cracked corn, and harvesting them later with the spike pole.

Many years later, lying in bed with an older woman, Tony was led to a comfortable conclusion about a grandfather who kills songbirds for food despite not needing to. He had given up trying to alter the fates of things in his life because plainly he was no good at it. He had not saved the pigeon. The most he had done was make it feel a bit more secure before it ultimately died an uglier death than the one he'd saved it from. And to alter the behaviour or thinking of a man like his grandfather would be as complicated and impossible as time travel.

His grandfather had been dead four years, and Tony lay on a lumpy futon in the bedroom of Ewa Loest, catching his breath after an early evening's lovemaking.

"Tony, I think about my own father, and what he has done since the war. How is it possible to enter the skin of someone like that and make him better? And who's to say what's better? If you are not like your family, it is because you have been differently tested. We live in an absurd time, this end of the century. We simply are different from them. You must let them remain back there where they belong. Don't try to bring them with you."

There would be more strenuous lovemaking later in the night, and yet more the next morning. Ewa, a visiting scholar from the Czech Republic, was a demanding and athletic lover. Their relationship would last little more than one spring and summer, and it would wear Tony out. By the end of their time together, Tony would have decided to stop trying to alter the lives of the young athletes he coached, and taken the well-paying desk job offered him by the League. Ewa was scheduled to leave Toronto to teach at a university in the States. When they began sleeping together, she told Tony he could expect nothing beyond the end of August, as she was to meet up with her fiancé at the new school. In her words, they were merely "helping each other through the summer."

Ewa was always interested in the ways people were tested

in life, and how they responded to testing. She studied and taught criminology, and applied scientific strictness to all human activities. Their first sex had been sudden and unplanned, though Tony had hoped for it for weeks before.

Ewa and Tony's affair began in early April. They met while both audited a philosophy night class on the ethics of decision-making. Walking through the back campus together one evening after a late lecture, they were caught in a sudden spring snowstorm. It advanced on the university from Lake Ontario, howling through the canyons of downtown Toronto and falling on top of them across the gothic roofs of Hart House and University College. The air filled with dry, icy flakes and, within minutes, curbs began to drift soft under the swirls of snow blowing across the roads. Ewa laughed and opened her arms to the storm.

"This, finally, is the Canada I imagined," she gasped in the force of the cold gusts, and turned to Tony, a spectacular shine in her eyes. "Please, take me somewhere wild."

Tony had known her just long enough to realize he had stepped into a test. In her head was a picture of some experience she expected of this country, or this city or this man, and now it was time for it to happen. He felt a jolt of despair pass through him. He wasn't ready for the test, hadn't expected it would arrive so soon, but he thought quickly nonetheless. The yellow glow of a vacant cab approached them across Hoskins Avenue.

"The beach," Tony found himself saying to the driver. "Queen and Woodbine, as fast as you can without killing us all."

He settled back into the seat and found his hand resting

between Ewa's. She was rubbing her palms together, warming herself up. The city passed in whiteness and grey washed with the yellow of street lamps, a short twenty minutes of silent drifting motion. Snowstorm acoustics blanketed the streets, and when they left the cab the mixture of sound under the muffle was the clacking of bare tree branches in the wind and a distant, low roar. They crossed Woodbine Park to the boardwalk. As he'd expected, Tony and Ewa were the only people willing to face the lake wind on such a night. To the west, the city blinked faded lights through a wall of white on black. The aerial strobes of the CN Tower sent out eerie, haloed glows. Lake Ontario bucked and roared in front of them, kicking up screens of icy spray to join the snow. It was the black heart of the storm, cold and deadly. It was exactly what Ewa wanted. She hopped on her toes on the boardwalk letting out screeching explosions of laughter.

"It's perfect." She screamed into the wind. "It is so unmistakable."

The beach was divided by impromptu juts of rock and concrete, craggy wave breaks that stretched like fingers far into the lake. Ewa pulled Tony by the hand out above the water, a six-foot width of broken and icy concrete between them and certain drowning. The sides of the breakwall grew softer the further out they went, rounded and smooth, the leftover shapes of millions of frozen waves, dripping stalactites between cracks in the rock. When they could go no further they turned back toward shore to see only the white torso of the storm, thickening now and twisting with its own gusts. The city also had disappeared. There was Tony and Ewa, and there was snow and water and ice. There was nothing else. Ewa pulled Tony's head to her mouth and spoke low into his ear.

"This is how we live," she said. "Threatened. If you brought me here, it means you understand this, yes?"

"Yes," he said, realizing, suddenly, that he agreed.

Ewa turned to look back out into the lake. Her black hair had a white gleam around it. Tony touched the gleam and it crackled. He ran his hand down her back, and it was like he was caressing a woman sculpted in glass. In the three minutes they were standing on the breakwall, they had been misted over by lake-spray. Every surface, including skin, held a thin, hard coat of ice. If they stayed still, they would eventually freeze in place.

At Ewa's apartment they dried their heads with towels and warmed the rest of themselves at the radiator.

"You are a perfect gentleman," she said, removing her wet clothing. "I asked you to do something for me, and you did the *best* possible thing."

Tony looked at her, shivering beside the radiator in a black bra and panties, rubbing the red skin of her legs with a towel. He understood that he had tested well. There was a brief struggle on the living room couch. The initial discovery of lips and tongues and skin, the testing of shapes in the hand. There were pauses in which they looked at each other, looked at bodies and fingers, and looked at the situation; pauses to assess and approve. In the bed, Tony was surprised by an actual growl. He looked at Ewa's face and realized another test had begun. Her arms tensed and her legs locked around him. He was being challenged to fight for control, and it was not a fight he might easily win. When he managed to enter her, she laughed with surprise and approval. They wrestled in this way most of the night. He woke in the morning to her encouraging hands and mouth preparing him for more.

"Tony, you worked so hard, and lasted so long for the first time with someone new. I'm very proud of you," she smiled. "But, I'm not finished, and it's very important that I finish. If I don't finish, I won't be able to do any work today. Do you think you can? Or shall I do it myself?"

Ewa Loest's need to finish would define Tony's life for the next few months. He found himself attending this need at all times of the day and night and in any place available. They made love on the creaking plywood desk in the tiny library office she'd been assigned at the university. They quickly and efficiently had sex in most of the bedrooms of host professors during a summer of dinner parties. One night in early August, Tony managed to help Ewa finish while floating in a moonlit Lake Rosseau at the cottage of a fellow graduate student. Only once during the whole of the spring and summer did Tony collapse in limp exhaustion, unable to bring it all to its conclusion. He lay in Ewa's bed while she kneeled on the mattress and finished herself with his hand. He watched her clenched eyes and marvelled at her determination. The sight of her finishing herself gave him new life, and the night ended well.

Thirteen

Tony wakes to the sound of horse's hooves on a road. The open window of his room lets in cool morning air, mist and the echo of horseshoes. It is before real light, when the air is blue. There is another sound, a piercing clank of steel on steel. This sound, and not the horse, has woken him. He pulls himself to the open window and looks out over a landscape that both rises and falls before him. Across the road, at the station, a lone man in a black overcoat walks the track beside a steaming passenger train. He carries a flashlight and a long steel hammer. He walks the length of the train, stopping at every wheel to tap and listen to the sound of steel ringing in the early morning. He is testing for weakness in the wheels. Beside Tony's bed, a large silver-plated trophy stands in a padded black carrying case. Tony opens and closes the clasp on the case and slips back into bed.

On the third weekend in June 1995, in the northern town of Ilisesti, Romania, there are two wedding ceremonies for the same couple, and the Cup is present at neither of them. On the Saturday, while a small civil ceremony takes place at the town hall, Tony keeps to himself, keeps close to the Cup, spends most of the day staring from his hotel room window into the wooded hills of Bucovina, into the soft hills speckled with sheep, and lush, forested valleys. He watches the comings and goings of trains at the station. He photographs soldiers and tourists walking the tracks and platforms. He uses his binoculars to discover birds in the tall pines surrounding the small tourist hotel.

The next day, at the church ceremony, Tony stands in a crowd of family, friends, reporters and onlookers as Dragos Petrescu marries Irina Mihu, a girlfriend from childhood, hardly even a woman yet, and someone with whom the young hockey player seems oddly formal. Tony wonders if the marriage has been arranged. The priest chants and speaks, guests hold golden crowns over the heads of the bride and groom; many people, guests and casual passersby, kiss a very large Bible. Every woman holds flowers, while fragrant beeswax candles light the stone walls and floor.

Children in rags stand near the entranceway, quietly begging and offering prayers for money. In another corner of the church, an older priest holds a private mass for the dead, one old woman in black standing before him in the gloom. In his mind, Tony recounts the number of times he checked the ancient lock on his hotel room door and feels the weight of the heavy iron key in his pocket.

The only Romanian citizen ever to win hockey's championship trophy, twenty-one-year-old Dragos Petrescu, a sudden, entirely unexpected national celebrity, has brought the Cup with him to his wedding. It is to be the centrepiece at the reception, set on a small podium behind the head table, to be used as a background for photographs; to be viewed, touched and admired by all the guests and visitors. Tony Chiello, the keeper of the Cup, keeps out of the way, eating tiny meatballs and Black Sea caviar, observing the traffic around the Cup. Occasionally he wipes down the trophy's gleaming sides with a silk handkerchief, to remove fingerprints and the grease of dinner, to make it perfect again.

There is dancing to mandolins, violins and clarinets. Gypsy music sings from the bandstand and women wrap their men in long scarves on the dance floor. In one corner of the hall, several older men in dark suits crowd around a small table. Smoke rises from them; they laugh and drink, slap backs and tug at the sleeves of each other's jackets. On the table, there is a game of backgammon. There is cheering for good dice and low, ironic murmuring for bad. Wooden pieces slide across the wooden board with force, are picked up and slapped down again. The groom sits at the table across from a man in his seventies. They smile at each other drunkenly, each smoking a long cigar. Tony assesses the board. The old man is clearly in front, and Dragos appears to be stalling, pointing at his own pieces and speaking quickly in his own language.

"He is explaining how the backgammon is like hockey."

A powerful hand grips Tony's arm, and he finds his glass refilling with champagne. Nicolae Petrescu-Nicolae, the hockey player's hulking father, has lurched across the room to accost and instruct Tony, drunkenly, joyfully.

"Soon he will lose this game, so he takes his time now to make this explanation."

Nicolae leans down on Tony, his gleaming bald forehead speckled with sweat, a cigar raging in his smile. He carries a bottle of champagne by its neck, drinking from it whenever he removes the cigar from his mouth.

"He is showing how the playing surfaces are very similar, a rectangle with a line in the centre separating all the action. Both games, you see, are essentially races, with the fastest player most likely winning the day, but both games also depend on a wise use of speed. There is such a thing as speeding to one's own destruction. Go too fast at the wrong time in hockey and you are offside, destroying a scoring opportunity. Concentrate only on the speed of your players around the board in backgammon, and you will spend all night on the bar, reading the newspaper, as they say. Like my idiot son himself has done tonight. But who can blame a man for going too quickly on his wedding night? You know what I mean, of course."

Dragos plays his bride's grandfather Andrei, a man whose abilities at the game have been tested every day for almost eighty years.

"The old man almost never loses, even when the dice are against him. He knows this board like a man knows the pattern of moles on his mistress's chest. He played backgammon against the Fascists in the '30s."

"Did he beat the Fascists?" Tony asks.

"He is here today, is he not? Of course he didn't beat the Fascists. He may be the best backgammon player in this country, but when the Fascists are in power, one does well not to beat the Fascists at any game."

The game ends as expected, with much cheering for old Andrei who clasps his hands together over his head and then runs to the podium to kiss the Cup. Everyone crowds around to take photos of the two champions, generations apart, posing with the trophy.

"You play?" Nicolae asks Tony.

"Mostly I watch, but I think I'm getting better at it." Tony searches the room quickly with his eyes, looking for Diana, hoping she will not notice him in conversation over a backgammon board.

"Then we will play. Please sit."

Tony sits across from the large, sweating man. The heat of hands and exertion rises from the table. Tony checks across the room for the Cup, safe in the arms of someone who won it. The party builds force around them, young and old dancing and singing, men standing in groups near the doorway, smoke rising from them as though from a campfire. Dragos Petrescu has seen his father sit down at the gaming table, and he sends Tony a stern nod.

"You are probably wondering why it is my son uses only his mother's maiden name?" the older man laughs across the table. "You know how this life is. You try to always live as though you are doing the best for everyone. Sometimes, you do not succeed. If you knew how we sacrificed for this boy."

Tony looks into Nicolae Petrescu-Nicolae's smiling, half-crazed eyes and the game begins.

Of course, very little the police could do to Nicolae Petrescu-Nicolae before he left Romania mattered to him. He was confident of eventually getting away. There was great pressure on the government at that time not to make immigration too difficult for genuine Jews who genuinely wanted to live in Israel. They could stall Nicolae in paperwork and bureaucracy for a few years while they tried to talk him out of it, but eventually they would have to open up the gate at the airport and let him go. At that time, planes were leaving every week for Tel Aviv. The truth of the situation was that there were not so many genuine Jews on those flights, and not so many people who genuinely wanted to go to Israel to live. Israel was the pathway to America, and America, meaning New York, was the ultimate destination.

The police were aware of the leaking hole in international convention, and it made them more zealous in their interventions into the immigration process. As a result, Nicolae had his two fellows assigned to him. Two officers who made it their business to be in the same places he was. The police especially liked to observe Nicolae on Jewish High Holidays. Naturally, when one is asking Israel to take you in, it is a good idea to be aware of the Jewish High Holidays, if not to observe them, at least to know which is which and not be wishing someone well at Yom Kippur when it is Rosh Hashanah. On the High Holidays, one of the two plainclothes men would always find some reason to invite Nicolae into the police station, an invitation he was obliged to accept. He spent many a Jewish High Holiday at the police station in Bucharest answering questions.

"So, Petrescu, I understand you like plum tarts?"

Nicolae would scratch his head, trying to discover if there was some Hebrew proscription against plums, or pastry, or enjoying sweets on holidays.

"Yes, I suppose I have eaten a tart or two in my life. They can be very enjoyable when baked well."

"Yes," they would say meaningfully, while writing something down in a small book.

"Did you see the result of this Saturday's derby, Petrescu?

Steaua gave it up in the eighty-ninth minute and it ended in a draw. Damned amateurs."

Here, perhaps, they were actually looking for sympathy, absurdly because Steaua was the football team of the Party, whereas Nicolae and his friends had always been for Rapid, the team of young fashionable dissenters. Nicolae would have been happy for a last-minute tie against Steaua in the derby, happier still if Rapid had beaten them 3-nil, but on matters of football he didn't fool around.

When football entered into the conversation, he knew he was no longer on the familiar ground of political or social disagreement. It was one thing for the police to be suspicious of your loyalty to the country, and for them to investigate you for dissent, but let them get a whiff of your sentiment in the arena of football and things could go very badly indeed. He would say it was a shame, and that Steaua should put so-and-so on the second team, or bring such-and-such off the bench. This is all he could risk, knowing so-and-so to be one of Steaua's best players in fact and such-and-such to be a complete incompetent. He risked this, knowing it was fine to be wrong in an opinion about football as long as you are talking about the correct team.

"Petrescu, why is it you buy your mineral water at the First of May, when you buy your salami on Dorobantilor? What is so special about the mineral water at First of May?"

"It is merely a question of routine. Besides, it is easiest for me to buy the mineral water closer to home as then I don't have so far to carry it."

"You sure, Petrescu? You sure you don't just like the looks of the girl who sells the mineral water at First of May? She's something to look at I think, but of course, I do not have a wife and child."

"Exactly Comrade Officer, you and I have different responsibilities, and so it only makes sense that you would notice this detail while I do not. If you say she is pretty, I will believe you, and maybe hazard a look next time—but only a look."

"Petrescu, did you do well in science at the gymnasium?"

The questioning would continue in this vein, often for two hours or more. Police and suspect together would smoke an entire pack of Carpați, the stubby, intensely fragrant Transylvanian cigarettes, sitting across the broad table from each other, with the mysterious table set in the corner doing nothing. Sometimes the officers would get up from their chairs, and without saying a word would leave the room. Nicolae understood at these times that he was to stay perfectly still, not leave his seat, and worry about what was to come. Whether this was a strict rule or not, it seemed the thing to do, and though he often felt lonely and anxious, there was always some kind of disturbance to concentrate on, some clicking from behind the walls or the sound of something scraping across the floor above his head. All part of the game, he could tell, but distracting in fact, and comfortingly banal in a way he was sure was not intended. The fear of what might be behind those sounds was obviously intended to disable him in some way, to suggest horrors he could then expand upon with his own imagination. And this he did, at first, but even horror can become familiar.

After the Revolution, Nicolae discovered, along with everybody else, what had always been suspected about the building he was taken to again and again. These people, these secret police, did indeed kill their own fellow citizens in that very building. They killed and maimed and ruined the minds of many, many people in that very building with the crazy backgammon game in one room. It is for this reason that many of the Securitate were dragged into the street and kicked to death by mobs during the Revolution. Many people were touched with real pain because of this building in central Bucharest and what went on in the rooms.

By the time it was his turn to get on a plane and leave Bucharest, Nicolae was no longer amused by the games he was forced to play. While the Securitate may not always have had the authority to hurt or kill, while they may not have been in a position to justify an outright disappearance, they were always able to place a threat on the table and leave it there. They were never without this option, as it was the simplest thing to do. Only they really knew whether or not they were prepared to follow it through. And when they got the threat right, it was an enormous burden on the mind. Sometimes they would not get it right and it would just seem ridiculous. Mostly, they succeeded.

Inevitably, they figured him out. Despite the fact that he did indeed escape to Israel, the Securitate won the little game they'd been playing before Nicolae left. They found the lever controlling his self-confidence and they used it. It was a matter of simple psychology. Their greatest success came not in actually catching Nicolae at anything shameful or illegal, but in presenting to him evidence that his sense of security had been compromised.

To live at all comfortably in such a police state, it was important to have something in your life that was completely secure and private. A man had to be able to walk down the street with a secret folded into his brain, and know it was safe. A man had to have at least one source of unwavering trust. He had to trust himself and anyone else who knew his secret. It was this essential trust that made it possible for entire generations to live without real freedom, because within this trust there was a kind of freedom.

Nicolae owned a radio. It was a small Grundig his father bought for him in Berlin during the 1950s when he was stationed there at the embassy. It was commonplace for diplomats and dignitaries to bring back electronics from the West, and it was not so strictly controlled in the 1950s as it was later. Western radios generally were not tolerated well, especially good German radios like the Grundig, which were capable of scanning the shortwave bands to pick up Western radio broadcasts. Nicolae's father knew that particular radio was capable of these things, but in his naiveté about his son, he did not imagine Nicolae would have any interest in such broadcasts.

Romanian citizens, even in the time of greatest strength for their Republic, when they depended so much on the friendship of the USSR, still they hated the Russians. The USSR would send touristing dignitaries to the Romanian countryside to hear Gypsy music, eat peasant food and treat the common people as their servants. If the tourists went away unhappy, soon they would return in tanks. That was the understood agreement with the Russians. In this environment, to hear someone from the West on the radio, someone not afraid of the Russians, to hear someone who might make a joke at the Russians' expense and not suffer their anger, it was pure romance. Many people, especially young people, found ways to enjoy the illicit shortwave broadcasts, and for a long time it was relatively safe entertainment.

When the People's Republic was strong, the government didn't worry about what was being said about them on Radio Free Europe. But when times were difficult, and they soon became so, then the radios became a problem. For a time the government blocked the signals of Radio Free Europe, the Voice of America and the BBC World Service. At some point they came to realize that almost anyone who could listen to these broadcasts was listening. And they weren't listening just to get the football scores from England, though these were very important. There had been some high-profile defections from the country. Before it was commonplace to listen to the BBC, Nicolae and his friends almost never heard about a defection, except through the street network if the defector was in any way famous; a poet or filmmaker for instance. But then, someone from the graduating class at the university, someone Nicolae himself had met on many occasions, Valentin Cescu, a hobbyist radio technician and sometime broadcaster on student music shows, went to the seaside and never came back.

A very short time later they began to hear Cescu's voice on their radios, coming through Voice of America. Now this, a young man so well-connected in Bucharest society, in fact a son of the Party, broadcasting back into Romania for Voice of America? This was too much for the government to tolerate. No longer could they scoff at the popular broadcasts as ignorant Western propaganda. Suddenly it was as though it were coming from directly inside the country. For them, it was nothing less than an intellectual insurrection. When Cescu satirized the powerful, he was able to use their names and popular nicknames. When he spoke of the imprisonment of the soul in Romania and the freedom to be found in West Berlin, it was all first-hand knowledge. And then, after speaking for a while, would he play some state-approved marches or patriotic folk songs as he had been directed to do when he worked in Bucharest? No, he would play the Mamas and the Papas' "California Dreamin.'" He would play the Rolling Stones' "Sympathy for the Devil." He would play Frank Zappa. And to sign off, he would say simply, "Cescu, ciao."

Right away the government set out to block his signal. The young people of Bucharest enjoyed a few weeks of hearing their friend on the VOA Romanian broadcast for two half-hours every day, and then suddenly nothing, static, just noise. It was a crushing loss for young people in Bucharest, and the beginning of even more exciting times.

It is the way with governments who would like to exercise complete control over the minds of their people, that they are often too easily satisfied in their small victories. It's true they managed to block the signal reaching Bucharest, but they could not manage to block it all over the country. Services like VOA and Radio Free Europe were aware of the government's transmission blocks, and were more than willing to build new transmitters at different border areas to try to slip their signal under the block. Soon, very soon in fact, it became known that the signal could be heard in Timisoara, a city very near the border with Yugoslavia. There was a rumour the US had sent a special ship into the Adriatic to blast the signal across. Crazy speculations like these abounded—special ships, special aircraft, livestock with transmitters in their coats. Crazy, impossible ideas, but wonderful fuel for gossip, and a new opportunity for the young in Bucharest.

Everyone knew someone in Timisoara, and eventually a network was arranged in which reel-to-reel tape recordings of Cescu's broadcasts were passed around Bucharest. Nicolae's group would arrange parties just to listen to the latest tape from Timisoara. Naturally, such activity was much more dangerous and risky than just listening to a radio program. A radio signal is the air, but a tape is something physical. A tape is evidence. Whereas, before the signal-block, listening to Cescu was simply a matter of closing the window so the neighbours could not hear; after the block, in the time of the tape network, there were tapes to be transported and hidden. An absolute trust in the network of like-minded friends became the one thing, the only thing. You did not lend the tape to anyone outside the network, and no one outside the network was to be aware of the parties at which the tapes were heard. Many networks existed already to share copies of banned books and pamphlets, and they were all extremely private things, dependent upon everyone in them being known to everyone else from a very young age. Otherwise, it would have been like handing the police evidence about yourself and your friends.

Among Nicolae's small group of friends, very few things were taken at all seriously, but this was one. Any disruption of the network caused immense concern with everyone. There was an instance when one of their group misplaced a particularly dangerous book that had been in his possession, a new collection of poems by a poet who had been exiled years before. It had been published by an expat press in Paris, and smuggled into the country by someone's father. The book was passed through Nicolae's group in a hurry, and it was hot, not something anyone wanted to hang onto for very long, because it contained plainly anti-government sentiment and no less than a call to arms for the Romanian people against their oppressors. Very poetic, very exciting, but too hot for the time and place. They agreed on a system in which each member of the network would keep the book only three days before passing it on, and once everyone had seen it, they would gather to burn it together. One of a few sad book burnings the friends, by necessity, had to perform over the years.

When it came time for Ion Lupescu to pass the book on, he was unable to produce it. In fact, it was revealed that he had misplaced it on the very first night he had it, and had been vomiting from nervousness for the two days since. This network was normally not very serious a group of people, the same boys in fact who would toy with the street police after curfew, a few close girlfriends and one or two trusted professors from the university. But this was an ugly scene. Lupescu wept when he finally revealed his error, and Nicolae went so far as to strike him across the face. It was not out of anger that he struck, but fear, a fear they all suddenly felt at the thought of the book being connected to them. A small group walked Lupescu back to his apartment, and set about searching. This was not an easy task, as Lupescu's parents and grandparents lived in the three small rooms of his apartment with him, and the network did not extend to members of family. There had been too many patriotic public betrayals of family members for any one of the young men to relax their guard at home.

Two of the group, Paul and Dan, were to distract the older members of the household with some chatter or other, to talk about the football match or some such thing, maybe to talk about some good fresh yogourt that was to be had at Dorobantilor market. These topics were always welcome in Bucharest at that time, and while they talked, Nicolae was to help Ion search the apartment for the book.

Their immediate assumption was that someone in the family had found the scandalous poetry and hidden it from Lupescu. This might be done for any one of many reasons. As a joke perhaps, though considering the nature of the book, it was not a very funny joke. Perhaps the book had been hidden from Ion out of fear; perhaps his mother had picked it up and, fearing her son would get himself into trouble with such a thing, had secreted it away. Most sickening, of course, was the thought that it had been taken as evidence and was right then in the possession of the authorities who were building a case against the little group of friends.

In the end, it was none of these. Knowing his friend to be susceptible to exaggeration, Nicolae suspected that rather than actually losing the book, Ion had merely hidden it away from himself through carelessness. He insisted Lupescu show him all the normal hiding places for such things in the apartment. In this time, every house and apartment in Bucharest contained any number of secret compartments and hiding places for the safe storage of whatever needed hiding away—religious icons, the inevitable stash of American dollars, compromising photographs and banned literature.

Lupescu showed him first the compartment he had fashioned beneath a heavy writing desk in the entranceway to his family apartment. Designed as a small and very narrow drawer beneath the back left-hand corner of the writing surface, the compartment hung from wire runners and could be completely removed and stashed beneath one's coat in a matter of seconds. In place, it looked exactly like a simple wooden corner support, and in fact Lupescu had built a solid support in the exact same style for the back right-hand corner, as a decoy for his compartment. The false support even contained screw heads on its surface to make it appear permanently secured in place. The great advantage of this spot was the speed and quiet with which things could be hidden away or removed from it. Lupescu insisted it was not possible either his parents or grandparents were aware of this spot, as he had built it while they were away on a seaside holiday years before. The lost book of poetry would just have fit into this tricky drawer, and in fact this had been the spot Lupescu had chosen for it, but it was not there.

Two other spots, a traditional loose floorboard in the bedroom and a very public inside ledge beneath the stairwell leading to the street, were also empty. Hiding contraband in a public place was also very popular as it could not necessarily be linked to whomever had hidden it away. The disadvantage, of course, was that one often lost one's contraband. This was the risk one took.

Lupescu was frantic as he showed Nicolae this last spot, having already conducted this exact search several times himself.

"You see," he cried, "someone has the book. It can only be in one of these three places. Someone has found it."

"Only these three—nowhere else?"

"I have only three places. What else do I have to hide?"

"What about temporary spots? I know when I am reading something I don't want my father to see, I often put it directly onto the bookshelf in the living room. There is one top corner of the shelf; it has only old German novels my mother bought in Berlin. He has no interest in these, so if I need a spot in a hurry, I slip a book behind these novels. Anything like that?"

"No," Lupescu moaned, "my grandparents are constantly rereading everything on the shelves. There is no safe place there."

At this moment, Nicolae had an inspired memory. He remembered a time he'd spent working with Lupescu in the north. Through a connection he had in the tourist office, Ion had managed to get them both summer employment as tour guides. They took East German and Russian tourists through the monasteries around Suceava, and stayed the entire summer in a hotel in Câmpulung.

One morning after a night of vodka with the Russians, Nicolae had a need that could not be postponed and he crashed through the bathroom door without knocking. Ion sat on the toilet, reading an Italian fashion magazine given to him as a tip from one of the female comrades. As Nicolae came through the door, intent on the toilet, he caught Ion in a position embarrassing for all men. Ion made a desperate attempt to hide the magazine from Nicolae. It was a standard large book of colour photographs of beautiful Italian models. What clothes they wore in these photos were wonderfully colourful and fashionable, but, in fact, they wore very little. To hide the magazine, Ion slipped it between the toiletry cabinet and the wall. The story of Ion's fashion magazine had become legend among Nicolae and his friends.

Nicolae excused himself to the toilet in the Lupescu apartment, and left Ion fretting in the drawing room, listening to Dan and Paul talk about yogourt. Indeed, there was a narrow space between the toiletry cabinet and the wall in this toilet as well, and there was the missing book of inflammatory poems. It had been flung far back into the space, as though in a terrible hurry, and was not readily noticeable from the toilet. Even had Lupescu remembered the possibility of this temporary spot, a spot he obviously used only in the most desperate moments, he might not have been able to see the book back there in the dark on first glance.

How the book came to rest in this spot, and why Ion forgot flinging it there, Nicolae did not want to know. He slipped the book into the inside breast pocket of his jacket and carried it with him out of the apartment. Only on the street did he open his jacket briefly to show Ion and the others that they had recovered the contraband. When Nicolae mentioned where it had been, Ion's face at first lost colour and then slowly adopted the shade of undercooked beef. At the time, the friends were all too relieved to spend much effort on embarrassing Ion, but for years afterward, his passion for poetry was often referred to, to his great shame and everyone else's great delight.

Because of this episode, the network's involvement with the tapes of Cescu's broadcasts was more tightly controlled. Rather then lending them around, the group appointed one person, Nicolae, to keep them safe and he was to bring them to parties and play them there. His preference therefore was to have parties at his own apartment. In that way, he would not have to travel with the tapes. With less than a week to go until he was to escort his wife and young son onto a plane and fly off to Tel Aviv, Nicolae was spending more and more time talking to his two Securitate at the station house in Bucharest. They no longer bothered with an excuse to pick him up on those last days. They were simply waiting for him a block from his office and he would walk with them to the station, the three of them commenting casually on the weather or the price of cigarettes.

It was a sad time for Nicolae. As much as he desired to leave Romania, to travel the world and eventually see places like Greenwich Village, Brooklyn, the blues clubs of Chicago and Saint Louis, as much as all that was suddenly within his reach, he was leaving behind everyone who had liked him and tolerated his bad behaviour, who had entertained him in his beautiful country made horrible.

What happens in such a circumstance, when the subject has not responded to all the previous stimuli and therapy, and instead continues to insist on leaving the country, on betraying the People, what happens is the tempo and focus of the game changes. Once the plane ticket is in hand, and the bags are packed, it is like the moment in backgammon when the two players have managed to safely move all their pieces past the other's pieces. At this point, it is no longer a struggle, but simply a race. Also, the intensity and quality of the game changes, as in a good endgame of chess when each player has little more than their king, a few pawns and perhaps one meaningful piece. Suddenly, moves are at once more forceful, less subtle, full of ultimate importance. No more room for error. Little hope for a sudden and unexpected reversal of fortune after a blunder. Make a mistake at this stage, and it means the game.

Nicolae's two police friends were no longer interested in convincing him to stay. He was leaving; they had accepted that. Their mission had changed, and they were now only interested in limiting the damage he might do from out of the country. There were no more suggestions that Nicolae was robbing his son of a homeland, and that he was unaware of the realities of life in the West. No more lectures about the plight of the blacks in the American south, or the destruction of entire races of North Americans for the sake of expansionist commerce. They had each of them lost and won parts of these little battles over the three previous years of afternoon meetings. Nicolae mostly allowed them to win the debates on ideology, since there was little to gain scoring intellectual points against men with such heavy fists. Occasionally, for his amusement, he would gently question assumptions, make them struggle for answers, but he never took the last word.

"I understand, Comrade," he might say, "the American Negro lives in a state of extended economic slavery. They are beaten into a subhuman existence by the cruelties of the profit motive. What I don't understand is why then are there so few Marxist American Negroes? Why is it we do not cultivate their oppression for our ends in extending the Revolution to the West?"

They would respond with an inevitable reference to Paul Robeson, as though one very well-paid entertainer sympathetic to Communist ideology could make a difference in a population in love with the idea of one day becoming as well-paid themselves.

Nicolae would nod and repeat, "Yes, Paul Robeson, I had forgotten," and they would write something down in his file. But these discussions were now long past. The question was no longer *would he leave?* but was now *what would he do once he had left?* It had become important to convince Nicolae that Romania's control over his life would continue once he had crossed the border for the last time. This last job was one of their specialties and, quite possibly, the thing they did best.

They succeeded by showing Nicolae a simple photograph and then uttering two small words. Three days before he was to leave, after a short talk about the Israeli treatment of Palestinians, one of the officers opened Nicolae's file, took out an eight-by-ten, black and white photographic print and placed it on the table in front of him. It was a photo of Nicolae, several years younger, on his birthday. He recognized the occasion immediately. In the photo, Nicolae was smiling the shy smile he put on whenever he received gifts. One of the gifts, plainly visible in the shot, was a reel-to-reel tape recorder.

This photo the police placed on the table in front of Nicolae. Then they both stood and left the room. On his way, the last of the two said "Miki, ciao."

Photographs are often used as devices for code in wartime and between secret societies. It is simply a matter of predetermined meaning, or a meaning that can be gleaned from one's understood intent. Imagine a revolutionary group working within a country for the overthrow of the government. Imagine this group works in blind cells who do not know each other, but who are being controlled by a central intelligence and who must be mobilized quickly and with little forewarning. This mobilization message must also be silent so as not to inflame suspicion among the authorities or give them advance warning of a coming strike. This can be accomplished by coding the message within an innocuous photographic image. A picture of a family picnic perhaps, where the order to strike appears as an apple in the centre of the picnic table. No apple means the attack has been called off, but if there is an apple, this is an order of immediate action. The very elements of the image have specific meaning, and if you speak the language of the photograph, the meaning is clear.

Nicolae's photo meant, for certain, the police were aware of the Cescu broadcasts and Nicolae's role in playing them for his small network of friends at parties. The photo, and their final words to him were meant to say *we know about the Cescu tapes.* All Nicolae's work to hide the tapes in the special hiding places, all his network's secrecy and all their pride at being so subversive, these things could be thrown away. None of these things were ever real, because plainly, the Securitate knew of the Cescu tapes.

But, there was more to be read in the image. It was a photo not just of Nicolae and the tape player, but of him, the tape player and his parents. Certainly there was no Cescu tape being played on the device when the photo was taken. This was taken the day he received the tape player, years before Cescu made his fateful trip to the seaside. Also, it was Nicolae's practice to keep the existence of the illicit tapes from his parents, as his father would have sniffed treason and his mother would have worried for his safety. Yet, there were his parents in the photo, smiling widely at him with the new tape recorder, the tape recorder they have just given their son, the son who will someday betray his country.

Here then the police were showing him the subtle consequences of his decisions. Here they were beginning to whisper to him. *You know your parents are not involved in this treasonous crime, and we also know your parents are not involved in this treasonous crime, but if we want to, we can make them involved. Yes, you are escaping our control, but if you doubt our continued power, please take a look at these two smiling people in the background, and know that you have given us control over them.*

This whispering would visit Nicolae every night until that Christmas morning in 1989 when he woke in his bed in Montreal to the sound of his wife shrieking from the kitchen, "They've shot him, the bastard, they've killed him and that bitch of a wife as well." They watched CNN all that day, watched Ceauşescu's body slump against the wall over and over.

There was a final message in the photograph, the most insidious suggestion, and the favourite message Securitate deliver. Nicolae sat alone in that room, listening to the clickings and scrapings behind the walls, staring at the photograph, trying to read its code, trying to decipher what it is they wanted to tell him. And then, like a sudden blow from behind, he remembered who took the photo. Because of course the photographer had been in the room at the birthday, he was right there in front of Nicolae, smiling as well and telling Nicolae to get that stupid look off his face. He was wearing the cream from the cake on his nose and getting a little too drunk on the ţuică he brought for the occasion.

He was the one who always brought a camera, and the

one who developed his own photographs in a small dark-room in the basement of his apartment block. He was the one who controlled so carefully the distribution of prints so they might never fall into the wrong hands. He was the trust Nicolae had in that small circle of friends he had known his entire life. And here he was, invisible but undeniably present in the police station in downtown Bucharest three days before Nicolae was to leave for Israel.

"On the plane to Tel Aviv, I tried not to think any more of the two fellows in the station back in Bucharest," Nicolae says across the backgammon board, wiping sweat from the top of his head with a balled handkerchief. "I tried not to think of the people I was leaving behind and the painful doubts I had packed into our luggage. I tried not to think about photographs and my good friend Petre Dobrescu, the smiling photographer. I remember pointing out the window for Dragos to look at clouds—the boy had never seen clouds from above. I held my wife's hand and smiled at the pretty Israeli stewardesses, hoping for a free drink. I tried to imagine what waited for us on the ground, and could not. I tried to watch the film they were showing, and again could not."

Tony listens to the older man intently, and just as intently he rakes the board with his eyes, trying to discover some strategic advantage, some way for him to win, but it seems impossible.

"Then, I noticed two men sitting in the centre section of seats. They were a row ahead of us, and they passed a match-box back and forth between them. One man would take the matchbox and shake it in his fingers, as though to shake up the matches, except whatever was being shaken did not sound like matches. That man would then slide open the box and both men would peer in. The one who had shaken the box would then say something in Hebrew, and both men would nod. Then the matchbox changed hands and the second man shook, peered, said something, et cetera, over and over again. I watched this strange procedure for a long time, and finally, overcome with curiosity, I left my seat and walked past them in order to see what mystery they were sharing. In the matchbox was a small pair of dice."

Late in the evening, the doors to the wedding hall are opened, sucking in gentle summer air and the scent of pines, a slow cleansing of cigar haze and the smudge of beeswax candles, the sweat steam of musicians and dancers. The celebration slows and calms, catching its breath and resting before beginning again. A lone violinist scratches a slow, romantic waltz. It is a time for touching hands and cheeks, for fixing hair and dresses. Old people sit down. Stories continue around the backgammon board. Tony and Nicolae play the fourth game of a match of five. Other men take notice and crowd around. A foreigner is holding his own in the national game. It's an oddity.

Spectator chatter weaves through the games, interrupts the stories. There is a general willing of the dice for Nicolae. There is laughing and swearing. Plates of food are brought to the players from the never-empty side tables. Tony eats the blackened skin of a young pig, killed that very morning and roasted whole over a firepit dug into the earth outside the reception hall. The delicacy is salty and rich with burnt oils. He eats anchovy fillets mashed into soft butter on fresh crusty bread, pickled cucumbers and pickled hot peppers all from the local farms. Finally, he is handed a candied plum from the orchard of Irina's father, one of few plums not used to make țuică. Țuica is in the air, the smell of it lifting from the forearm skin of all the men crowding the table.

Diana appears behind Nicolae, shy at first around so many men who knew her as a child, but with laughter and țuică, heartened into joining the profane cheering. Her face is flushed from dancing, a greenish-tan dress open at the collar, a neck slick with perspiration. She looks away from Tony's eyes, and smiles at everything. He remembers how he caught sight of her in the plum trees earlier in the day, picking the fruit that will become next year's țuică. She had been seated in the upper branches, as though in the balcony of a theatre, carefully twisting the ripened plums from the branches, rubbing each one in both hands to test the firmness. At that time as well she had looked away from his eyes, and smiled. She had brought each plum to her nose, closed her eyelids and inhaled deeply.

The men notice Tony noticing her. There is a roll of laughter and Diana's face glows brighter in the candlelight. She yells back at the men, spitting fire, and they laugh even louder. Tony loses the game, stuck on the bar reading a newspaper while Nicolae quickly clears his perfectly blocked house. The match stands at two games apiece.

"My dear niece. She has been challenged to kiss you if you win. She has agreed, but I don't think you want to know what she said about you."

Nicolae smiles at Tony from across the board and scratches

at his goatee. He lights another cigar and picks up the dice.

"Do not think she wants to. She's just responding to a dare from the men. She cannot resist a dare. It is my job to make sure she does not have to kiss you. Please, nothing personal. For the honour of my niece, you understand."

"I understand." Tony says, but he has a physical memory of Diana's lips and, caught in a fog of drink and borrowed joy, he feels a need for more.

Another loud roll of laughter from the circle of men, and finally, Diana looks directly at Tony. She is defiant, proud. She sticks out her tongue and places both hands on her uncle's shoulders. Everyone slaps Tony's back at once. The bone dice clatter on the board.

"Six and six, the emperor's opening." Nicolae winks and sets up two solid blocks at the bar. Diana cheers and claps her hands, spins on her toes. A full glass of țuică slides across the table to Tony.

"You will need it, for the disappointment."

Unable to catch up in the race, Tony satisfies himself with blocking his house and holding two men back in the desperate belief they'll have a chance at a capture. A strategy of last hope, a prayer to the dice. When the roll comes, it feels as nothing other than a gift of fate. Nicolae is on the bar and trapped. Diana shrieks and tries to run away, but several men catch at her flailing arms and hold her in place, cursing. The match ends, three wins to two for Tony. Tony drinks his glass of țuică at once and sits back in his chair. In the crowd of men he recognizes Dragos smiling at him. Dragos raises a glass to him and drinks as well.

"Let her go if she wants to go," Tony offers. "Winning is enough."

Nicolae stands and holds his niece's hand.

"I'm sorry Diana. There are worse bets to lose, believe me."

"She's just embarrassed," Dragos laughs, "because she knows she can't do it without liking it."

His arm suffers for the joke. Diana's fist flies through the crowd, bruising him.

"Tony, you'd better hope she doesn't kiss like she punches. Not this time at least."

And his other arm suffers.

Tony feels his chair being lifted beneath him. He is turned from the table into the spreading crowd. Diana walks from the edge of her friends and relatives, suddenly onstage. She turns her back to Tony and curses the laughing crowd. When she turns back, she is smiling. She slips off a long silk scarf she has tied around her waist, and twirls it into rope between her hands. It feels cool on the back of Tony's neck, then suddenly tight and hot. Diana lands on his knees and draws him into her lips with the scarf.

The kiss is violent and contemptful. The heat of her forehead crushes into his ear. As she begins to pull away, Tony tastes her tongue on his, a final flash of anger, delicious and warm. To Tony, his reward seems to last much longer than the couple of seconds Diana gives him. The scarf slides from his neck and trails along the floor as she walks away lashing out with her fists at the drunken, hysterical crowd. They part to let her pass and Tony, confused and humiliated, watches her walk past the small podium where the Cup has stood since the party began. The podium is empty.

Fourteen

"It is an interesting feeling is it not?"

Nicolae Petrescu-Nicolae follows Tony from room to room in the wedding hall, up great wooden staircases and through narrow back corridors, checking behind pieces of furniture and inside darkened doorways.

"This feeling of suddenly not understanding anything. Language is always a difficulty in these situations. Not knowing the words. But worse I think is that sudden shock, that instance of ultimate strangeness. An experience all travellers have, even the bravest of us, I think, and certainly something all immigrants must eventually face. Whether it comes on the first day or the fifteenth or the five hundredth, there will come this moment when everything that once seemed normal and familiar and correct is whisked away like the tablecloth in a magician's trick. It is unsettling, isn't it?"

Tony walks with purpose ahead of the older man, vaulting stairs two at a time despite a head filled with homemade liquor. He calculates the time between his last seeing the Cup and the empty podium to be mere seconds. It is simply not possible that whoever took the trophy was able to get it very far. He knows his best chance of recovery will be if the Cup has been kept in the building. A quick look out the front door showed quiet empty streets and no signs of recent activity. He'd scanned the faces in the crowd to see if their eyes led him anywhere obvious, but the other guests, amused by his desperation, simply smiled back at him and laughed privately among themselves. Now it is simply a matter of checking every room in the building. The Cup will be found.

"It is my burden," Nicolae continues, undisturbed by the speed of their search and the fact that Tony is not listening to him, "that I brought this moment not only upon myself and my wife, but upon a young child. We are told children are very resilient, that they recover from trauma. What we are not told is that whether they recover or not is immaterial. Trauma is trauma. It is my burden, and I accept it."

The entire time they lived in Israel, Nicolae and his young family tried to leave their new and foreign homeland, tried to escape again to one of three places. Their preferred choice, of course, was the United States. Everyone wanted to go to the United States.

"To fly in an airplane over New York City," Nicolae says with a dismissive wave of his hand in the smoky air above his head, "to look down upon the Statue of Liberty and et cetera. You know the whole story. You don't think you are going to fall for this story, but when you have left the only world you know, and you must choose a new world, all of a sudden this story is very convincing. Next there was

Canada, which was also attractive if only because it is so close to the United States. The third and least attractive option was Australia, a great country to be sure, but so lost and alone there in the middle of the ocean. So far from anything we might understand, and with no accompanying story of its own.

"Naturally, it was Australia who made us the first offer. Australia opened her arms and welcomed us, and to this day I cannot say if we didn't make a terrible mistake by not opening our own arms in turn and running to Australia. In Montreal, on a morning in February when I am waiting for the bus on Sherbrooke, I am certain that Australia is laughing at me for my foolish decision. But, at the time we decided to wait."

The offer from Australia was open for three months, and Nicolae and his wife decided to wait the three months to see if they would also get an offer from the US. Very near the end of their wait they heard from Canada, or at least from Quebec. They decided not to stretch their luck any further, accepted the chance to become Quebecers and signed their names. They flew to Montreal with a map of North America spread between them across their knees, studying the terrain. They took note how, on their map, Montreal was not very far at all from New York City. They consoled themselves in their decision by measuring the distance between Montreal and Manhattan with their fingers.

The sky was clear and they could see everything as the plane came in over the country. They crossed Newfoundland and followed the Saint Lawrence River west into the land. It was all so big and empty, and they could imagine, looking to the south past the Berkshire Mountains, that it was also almost all New York City. It was early in October and the land was knit through with fantastic colours. They strained their eyes across the brilliant carpet, peering south, imagining they might see the tip of the Empire State Building peeking out above the horizon. And then the plane was on the ground and they were moving through the airport with everything they owned, never knowing to whom they should speak French and to whom English. They guessed at this speaking game, and guessed wrong almost every time.

That first night, in all the exhaustion of a day of travel, the luggage and the jet lag and the emotions of his wife and little Dragos, Nicolae was unable to keep his eyes closed in their tiny YMCA room. He would lie down and listen to his wife and child breathe, but then he would have to stand up and go to the window. At that time in Montreal, the YMCA sat directly above Boulevard de Maisonneuve. The traffic of the thoroughfare flowed through the building, cars and taxis on their way across the city, beautiful young people walking through on their way to Crescent Street clubs or going east for food at Ben's or to the jazz clubs of Saint-Laurent and Saint-Denis. And Nicolae was at the window, not knowing any of these places, but knowing at least that the blood was flowing, seeing it below him and feeling it hum up into his feet. There was so much kissing. So many arms clutching other arms. It was a fine show, too inviting, but he couldn't bring himself to go for a walk because the thought of his wife and child waking to find him not there was painful to him. After everything they'd just been through, he could not risk them waking up alone, without their only reason for being in such a strange place.

As morning grew in the window, Nicolae was surprised

by a knock on the door of the room. It was a quiet knock at first, respectful of the hour, and Nicolae was initially unsure if he was hearing it correctly. Their small room was one of many in a long hallway of identical drab grey doors. He was still standing at the window, watching the streets fill with daylight, and he looked over at his wife, still in bed but staring back at him now. They questioned each other with their eyes for many seconds before whoever it was knocked again, this time with more force.

A man was laughing now behind the door. Nicolae imagined the visitor had mistaken their room for that of a friend. He opened the door, again uncertain of which language to try, and looked at a small man dressed for cold weather shuffling slowly from foot to foot at the threshold. The unexpected visitor greeted Nicolae in his own language, by his own name, smiling broadly.

"I saw your name on the list of new arrivals downstairs," the laughing man said. "I knew you would be awake. I must tell you, to have you here in this city with me is the most beautiful gift. The most beautiful gift."

Without introduction, he handed Nicolae a small rectangular package, something Nicolae did not fully understand at the time but which he came to know as Canadian-style cookies, dry and too sweet with chocolate like wax, crumbling to the table every time he took a bite. The man waved to the small table and he and Nicolae sat.

"To begin," the man said, "please do not be afraid or concerned in any way. I am here as a friend. I hope to prove this to you."

Nicolae glanced again at Veronica in the bed. Dragos lay beside her, his eyes still closed, but his breathing betraying the fact that he was awake and listening carefully. The past year had prepared them all for almost any experience but this one. This one was new.

"You were mine," the man continued. "My very first, and my favourite."

Having said this, the man fell silent, and his laughing mood turned sombre. Nicolae sat across the table from him, munching cookies expectantly, wishing he had some coffee. He was aware of a growing tension between himself and the stranger as though already they had run out of things to say to each other, as though there was little more about the man that he cared to know and little more about himself that he cared to have known. It was a feeling he recognized, but vaguely, like the recollection of pain from far in the past.

It was Veronica, dressing herself behind a makeshift curtain wall, who first made the connection. She stuck her head out into the room and stared suspiciously at the interloper.

"We know nothing anymore," she said, her voice shaking with anger and fear. "We don't want any trouble. Why have you found us out like this?"

Recognizing severity in his mother's voice, Dragos ceased feigning sleep and raised his head to observe the growing drama of an unwanted stranger in a strange room in a strange country. The man suffered Veronica's questions like they were aimed at his face. His eyes filled with water and he could only look down at his hands shifting uncomfortably on the tabletop.

"I understand what I have done here," he said. "I'm sorry. I thought maybe the cookies, somehow... if you will please allow me a few minutes to explain myself. I assure you, I bring no trouble to your door."

JOHN DEGEN

The stranger's name was Alexandru Ionescu and, as Veronica had guessed, he was a member, a former member, of those very same secret police, the Securitate who haunted Nicolae's final years in his homeland. So it was, Nicolae Petrescu-Nicolae had left Bucharest, lived for over a year in Israel, travelled all the way to Montreal and on his very first full day there, he would have yet another talk with the secret police.

Veronica was not to be consoled. At the time, so early on her first day in a new country, she had become very unhappy and wanted this uninvited man to leave. Nicolae too could not see any reason to continue the conversation, except that this Alexandru Ionescu did not act like any police he had ever known. He did not seem concerned to prove to Nicolae that he was in charge, or that he was as smart as anyone else.

Underneath his genuine distress at having made a startling admission, he seemed, simply, very happy, like a child is happy. He watched young Dragos struggle to eat one of those bad cookies and laughed at the expressions on his little face. He looked around the room and out the window at Montreal, rubbed his moustache and said things like "fantastic; is it not fantastic?" while the wary family sat at the small table, looking at him, waiting for things to turn worse and wondering why they hadn't turned worse already.

It occurred to Nicolae that had he wanted to, this Alexandru Ionescu could have broken their spirits completely as soon as he entered the room, but he did not seem to want their spirits broken. In fact, it seemed this man had decided it was his job to make sure their spirits remained intact. As well, Nicolae could not ignore the fact that a Romanian Securitate in Canada simply cannot have the same powers as in Bucharest, and that in fact, if Nicolae had wanted to make trouble for this Ionescu, he may very easily have done so. *Former* Securitate, as this man claimed to be, were not generally in the habit of admitting to their past profession. It was the kind of history one generally wished to bury. For this man to make his admission to Nicolae was, as far as he could tell, a form of confession, not intimidation. Where Veronica's well-trained nose smelled trouble, Nicolae sensed only pathos. Ionescu saw this understanding cross Nicolae's face and continued his explanations.

Ionescu had worked for the state police in Bucharest since his days as a student. He had been recruited secretly at the university—this was one way the state kept track of the goings-on of so-called radical student activities—and he had been a very willing and enthusiastic recruit. As a young man he proudly infiltrated and then destroyed numerous secret networks just like Nicolae's own banned literature network, sending a small but significant number of his fellow students to jail for four years here and five years there. The number of his victims grew so significant that his presence at the university quickly became ineffective.

Students would begin to instinctively avoid these fellows, smelling prison on their clothes. Eventually, these agents would disappear from the university, pulled in by their police masters and reassigned to a place they could once again be effective. And then, of course, students like Nicolae were in worse trouble, because without the obvious mole, they had to wonder who the new well-hidden agent was.

They were more anxious without these operatives around than they had been with them in plain view.

Ionescu told the Petrescu family all about himself freely, though often he stopped his story to repeat an apology. It seemed to be an apology he had been developing within himself for a very long time, and to Nicolae's well-trained ear it contained a clear tone of sincerity. Ionescu said, "Please allow me to tell you about my former self, and so reveal my great shame again to the world," and sometimes, in the middle of his story he would just stop, rub the table-top lightly with his knuckles and say "my great shame, my great shame." Listening to this repeated *mea culpa*, Nicolae understood his first morning in Montreal was becoming extraordinary, and he began to enjoy himself.

Pulled from the university, Ionescu was sent for surveillance training in Timisoara, where he spent two years becoming the kind of secret police most feared in Romania. He became an invisible man. And when he said the words "invisible man" to Nicolae, the mystery of his face disappeared. In an instant, Nicolae understood the strange familiarity of his presence, how his body seemed to fit into the picture of the world as seen from Nicolae's eyes. Here was the man who had haunted him the last five or so years of his life in Bucharest. No longer the apparition on the periphery, here he was right in front of Nicolae, across a table in Montreal now, eating cookies with his family. It was a thunderous realization, one that made Nicolae leave his chair and back away from the table.

"You must understand," Ionescu said, rubbing his moustache, "with you it was always just play. I did not detect in you any real threat to the state. In my job, you develop a very dependable sense for these things. But I was a man who followed the orders handed down to me. I could question the logic of these orders in my mind, but not openly to my superiors. For some reason, they were worried about you, especially after you applied for a visa, but for me, I could tell you were not interested in counter-revolution. When you spent hours in the library of the American Embassy, it was just to read books from another culture. That is all, am I right? You simply love to read books. I watched you read so many books, Nicolae."

Ionescu was assigned to Nicolae, not in the way the other two fellows were assigned to him. Those Securitate were to make themselves known to Nicolae, to appear to him as police, to look menacing, and to occasionally invite him for a discussion at the station. Nicolae was to know these men when he spotted them, and to feel the weight of their oppression on him at all times. But there were three agents on Nicolae, not two, and Ionescu was the *invisible* man. It was Ionescu who let the other two agents know where Nicolae would be and who he'd be with. Ionescu gave them the information that allowed them to ask Nicolae such pointed questions. He was the invisible man who watched Nicolae eating plum tarts.

Ionescu was with him all day, every day. Nicolae was his job for over five years. He was to follow him through Bucharest, track his movements, anticipate any odd changes in routine, make note of his social circle, flag friends of his who were also worthy of individual surveillance. He was to follow Nicolae on his vacations and business trips especially, because it was on these disruptions of normal routine that most counter-revolutionaries did their real business. He was to do all of this without being detected.

"Once, Nicolae, I served you and your friends beer for an entire evening," Ionescu confessed, in Montreal, smiling with cookie crumbs in his moustache, "from behind the bar at that little tavern in Brasov. You were there for a conference, you remember. Some conference, Miki. How you can concentrate on work when you are throwing up half the morning I do not know, but it was all very entertaining for me. You see, it was a matter of playing for me, a matter of being able to look you straight in the eye as I handed you a stein of beer, to smile and know you had been fooled again. Fooled by me. And you, with your foolishness and gamesmanship that I admired so much. To be able to fool you was the greatest achievement."

Ionescu sat up straight at the table, smoothed his moustache and tried to calm the nervous tapping of his fingers on the tabletop.

"Nicolae," he said, a trembling of respect in his voice, "Mrs. Petrescu-Nicolae and the little sir, you have no reason to trust me, I know, but I wish to say to you that I am no longer a member of the security police of the Socialist Republic of Romania. You have nothing to fear from my presence here in your little room, just as you, Nicolae, never *really* had anything to fear from me in Romania.

"If you were going to practise counter-revolution in Romania, you had me completely fooled. You know, sir, you and all your friends would read Kafka, you would pass these banned books between you. You would smuggle in writings by that rogue Havel in Czechoslovakia, you would listen to your tapes of Cescu broadcasting on VOA. But what you did not realize is that your oppressors were reading the same things. How do you suppose such writing becomes banned? In so many ways, Nicolae, during those five years, you were a teacher to me. I would slip your books out of their hiding spots when I knew I had a day or two before a pickup. I would read what you read. In Romania, I began my job by thinking of you as a mark, as my target, yet by the time you left for Israel, I had come to think of you as a brother in absurdity. So, if you please, all of you, I am here in this room as a friend, and as someone seeking forgiveness and a new life of my own."

So formal, so dramatic. His speech was in the exact tone Nicolae had come to expect from a member of the ruling party proclaiming some important truth about the great socialist revolution, but the words were all wrong for who he was. He was being sincere about the wrong sentiments for a man like him. He was being, for him, *dangerously* honest. Nicolae and Veronica heard the new and strange tone behind what he was saying, and it made them more nervous still. What an entirely absurd land they had found if it could turn an Ionescu from what he was to what he now appeared to actually be.

"It was the watching of you, in fact," Ionescu continued, "that made it possible for me to be here today, I mean *in my own head* possible. I cannot say you convinced me of anything about our former country. I'm not really sure I ever needed convincing. Police work was a job to me. The job I was best at, and it had very little, I think, to do with politics or ideology. My great shame, my very great shame.

"I was good at following, good at reporting what I saw, very good at disappearing into a crowd and pretending not to be who I am. I see you are thinking I am probably still very good at pretending, and that is why you don't trust me. Fair enough. You should not trust me, but maybe you should trust where it is you are. This is no longer Bucharest. I have no authority here. If you wish, you can tell me to leave and according to the law of this country, I must leave. All I mean to say about my being here now, in Montreal, is that it seemed to me if you were so convinced there was a better life for yourself outside Romania, then the world outside Romania was not *without* interest to me.

"I admired you, Nicolae. Admired your mind, and the way you enjoyed your life. It is not logical that someone like you would take his family into a mistake. I was happy enough in Romania, but after you left, suddenly I understood that there was also something *not* in Romania. After your departure at the airport—did you see me there, Nicolae, selling flowers in the terminal?—the world was no longer small enough to fit within the borders of one small country.

"I don't think I would have left Romania, myself," Ionescu continued, "but for the next man I was assigned to. Such a dull, stupid man. He was a writer, this fellow, and he was a different sort altogether. I think perhaps he really was involved in counter-revolution. In half a year, I was able to report at least a dozen secret meetings with others under high suspicion. This man took me to Yugoslavia, and all the way to very near the border with Trieste. You and I understand what it means to be near the border with Trieste."

Ionescu mentioned the writer's name and Nicolae laughed. This poor writer, Stihi, must have been the unluckiest man in Romania. He was universally despised by the young intelligentsia as a mouse of the Party, his writings ridiculed and parodied in the underground alternative press, and somehow also he managed to attract the attention of the security police. This poor Stihi couldn't win.

"Stihi was invited to a conference of socialist writers in Belgrade," Ionescu explained. "You understand, the usual, 'cooperation between sister republics, for the good of the worldwide revolution' and et cetera. Whatever he must put down on his visa application—and of course officially, he was a member of the Party and above reproach, so such a trip would not be unusual for him. He was given the visa without problem, but he didn't realize there was a ghost on his trail. I was sent to Belgrade with him, inside his pocket. My God these writers, Nicolae, how they can talk the shit in a bar. Excuse me, young sir. How they can stroke themselves and love themselves and lick themselves all over with their tongues, each one in turn while the others listen and try to think only of their own superiority."

"Those unending evenings listening to self-congratulation and petulant competitiveness. How I missed you and your gang on those evenings in Belgrade. How I longed for someone to accidentally light the tablecloth on fire, or pretend to the waitress that they were officials from a Russian delegation, just to try and get free beer. There is no amusement in watching a gang of writers loving themselves in a bar. There is no life there, only the slow drip-torture of perpetual ego."

Nicolae was not surprised to hear this description of Stihi away on a conference. It is how he had always imagined the "Party writers" behaving. So full of themselves and their position with the ruling class. So unconcerned that their talent was being used as nothing more noble than the grease they apply to lubricate the tracks of tanks. So boring.

He was not surprised by the story, but he was surprised to hear it from this Ionescu. It was at this point of his long visit that Nicolae began to feel the first true easing of his spirit. As in Romania, the greatest clue someone was a friend and not a spy of some sort was the sympathy you felt for them when they spoke unguardedly. It was perhaps a foolish way to decide things, but for Nicolae it was often the only way to extend your trust.

"As with all conferences of this sort," Ionescu continued, "there must be the inevitable trip to the seaside, but instead of Dubrovnik, these morons are set to go north to Koper, in the Gulf of Trieste. I am sure the appearance of this trip to Koper on the official itinerary was part of the overall suspicion surrounding the man. Why go to plain, dull Koper over beautiful Dubrovnik with its girls in bikinis, unless there is some other reason you need to be so near the Italian border? As you must know, it is impossible I'm sure even today to go to Koper without there being at least one or two invisible men on your trail. The fleshly temptations of Dubrovnik are acceptable to the Party, but the temptations of Koper are worrisome."

Nicolae knew at least two others who had managed to slip across that very border spot. At that time, in 1985, it was considered one of the safest crossings. He had considered it as an option for himself once during an international handball tournament, but could not bring himself to make the crossing. The thought of leaving his family behind was too much for him.

"We were there just two days. The writers visited the beach; they walked together along the strand and no doubt talked some more about how wonderful they all were. They visited the local museum, took in some architecture and stayed, here now is the interesting part, they stayed in a hotel very near the train station. The train station, you understand. This was it, I was sure. If not Stihi, then someone in the group surely was going to make a crossing. Someone was going to slip from the hotel in the night and walk to Italy. It was possible and had been done before. So, I was a good little policeman and I went to the station to investigate the lines. I showed my papers to my comrade Yugoslavian security police officers and asked for access to walk the fences. I was assigned a young man to accompany me. You understand, there is no trust even among fellow security police.

"It was night and we were walking the perimeter fence. My comrade officer was explaining to me, in Russian, of course, that it was not true there had been many recent crossings there. This was a lie spread throughout the socialist world to embarrass Yugoslavia, long despised by its socialist sisters for its friendly independence from the USSR. These words all in Russian, you understand. He told me that the security at the railway border point was the highest it had ever been, and the whole time he was telling me this, I was watching the approach of a very obvious hole in the fence in the darkness between two light standards. There, almost a kilometre from the station, someone had dug a small dip in the earth beneath the perimeter fence right at the point where the light disappeared in a murky greyness.

"I pointed out the hole to my comrade, and at first he did not know how to respond. He wanted to blame it on an animal. Perhaps a dog had dug his way to Italy. For me, it was all very comical, but I contained myself and did not laugh at the poor struggling idiot comrade. Finally, my young guard gained control of himself and remembered something about procedure. But not enough about procedure, lucky for me. He *should* have used his radio to call for an investigative unit to come in their Jeep and fill in the hole, or even just to monitor it from afar and see who tried to use it. He should have, but instead he ordered me to stand guard at the hole while he ran back to the station to rally his fellows."

Ionescu smiled across the table at young Dragos, no longer sleepy-eyed but listening intently to the story, worried suspense on his young face. Nicolae also looked at his son and thought, "For him, this will always be just a story. That is my gift to him." Ionescu continued.

"A kilometre he would have to run, my young security escort. I heard his footsteps disappear in the night. Maybe I should have suspected a trap, but I didn't. And so there I stood, in the darkness, beside a hole from Yugoslavia to Italy, from east to west. The idea that I should leave then was upon me the instant my friend took his first running step, and I believe I hesitated not from fear or indecision, but simply to savour the moment when I became completely free.

"And I don't mean this slippery Western idea of freedom you will hear so much about in this new land, Nicolae. I mean, in that moment, when my comrade idiot security officer ran away from me in the night, I was completely free to make a decision in a way I had never before been free. I could choose to be who I had always been, to do my job and eventually to collect my pension, or to change completely into someone I suspected I might be. People will tell you this kind of decision is always possible here in the West, but don't believe them. It is only ever *really* possible when what is on the line is your blood. Your blood seeping slowly into the dust of some Yugoslavian border crossing—or for you Nicolae, your blood on the back of a chair in the Securitate offices in Bucharest, am I correct? That is when real freedom occurs. This uninvited guest arrives, this *choice*, bringing with him danger and the possibility of something fantastic and unknown. Then, and only then is freedom real.

"I love this new city, this Montreal, but I am not fooled into thinking it is so much more free than where we've come from, my friends, only that I was free in choosing it. You will see what I mean, I think, when you get your first jobs over here. You will see what this Western freedom really means.

"And now I am here. I made my coat a little bit dusty, then walked across, I think, fifteen sets of tracks in the switching area, and found the corresponding hole in the fence on the Italian side. A much more accommodating hole, the Italian hole. There were no shots, and no sirens. No bright lights switched on to blind me in my tracks. I simply strolled through the night into Trieste. You know, it is interesting about the tracks. I walked across them without counting them, not even thinking to, and only many weeks after my arrival in North America did I think back to that moment and wonder how many tracks there were. I can count them in my mind now, every one of them. The mind *knows*; it knows even when we don't, like you knew when you saw me outside your door. You *knew*. Your mind just took some time telling you. And now I am here. And, to my great joy, and my shame, so are you. Welcome, my friends, to my city. Welcome to Montreal."

That was it for him on that first morning. Ionescu came into their room with his terrible cookies, told them the story of his life for almost an hour and, just as suddenly as he arrived, he left. But before leaving he insisted on giving them one more gift.

"I have been in this Montreal for almost a year now," he said. "It is very different for defectors, you know, than it might be for just you everyday refugees. Defectors get a certain privilege; especially defectors these Western authorities think might be able to help them with information. From Trieste, I travelled quickly to Paris and London and, given the choice to stay in England or go to North America, with a list of 'safe' cities for me to disappear into, I chose Montreal. I chose this city, Nicolae, because I am still good at what I do. I knew you would not find in Israel what it is you need, and I knew how hard it was to reach New York. I bet against Australia for you, and... look at you here. I bet correctly.

"There are many Romanians here in Montreal, you will find. Many from recent times and many more from a hundred years ago. You know, they have a street in this city named after our Queen Mary, our teenaged English Saxe-Coburg who married Ferdinand. Everyone assumes it is named for a Scottish woman, but if you check the archives, it was named for our lovely Mary.

"And now, I am here. Still an invisible man. Now, I am invisible to avoid being followed myself, to save my own skin. It's almost too silly to think about. There is nothing I know that will help anyone perform any act of counter-revolution against great mother Romania or the Soviet Union, but I don't fool myself. I am Securitate, and the defection of a Securitate is serious business. Given the opportunity, they will try to kill me, I know this.

"Of course, this means I should not be talking to you—for my own good I should avoid the very sight of you; but, when I saw your name on the list, I simply could not stop myself. This is the new life, Nicolae. In the old life, I could never have spoken to you, I mean really spoken to you as I have today. But this now, what you see outside your little window here is the new life. I will not have to hide forever.

"Anyway, I will go now. I leave you these tickets. They are not much of a gift, but they are what I can afford to give right now. I think maybe you will enjoy this spectacle, maybe especially the boy here. It is no football match, but it is interesting, and more importantly, it is Canadian—from the new life."

Ionescu left the room before Nicolae could stand up from the table, closing the door for himself without looking back. Nicolae, Veronica and Dragos were left sitting at the little wooden table in the YMCA on de Maisonneuve, and on the table in front of them lay Ionescu's parting gift. Three tickets to the Montreal Forum for that very evening. Three tickets to see the Montreal Canadiens play hockey against the New York Rangers. One day in their new city, in their new country and they found themselves preparing to attend a sporting event. They didn't know what the Montreal Forum was, or where it might be in the city. Nicolae was familiar with hockey, of course. There had been hockey in Romania for many, many years, but as far as he knew it was played only in the very coldest time of winter, outdoors, and then not very well.

They had just been visited by a phantom from their old life. The most fearsome kind of phantom, a security police, and yet somehow none of them had succumbed to anxiety. They found themselves laughing about it. A security police had visited them, brought horrible cookies, made a confession and then left them with tickets to see a sporting match.

Nicolae and his family dressed themselves as nicely as they could manage, and went to the Montreal Forum to experience this spectacle Ionescu had promised. The tickets were for 7:30 in the evening, a strange time for sports. Would it not be dark? Before the game, they did their business for the day. It was important they checked in at the immigration department and made their various appointments with advisors and assistance agencies. There were distant connections, the friends of friends, the relatives of relatives to be telephoned and surprised with a friendly voice in their old language. And, of course, there was the city to be explored, an art gallery here and there, a subway system to be deciphered. They were told by one of the friends of friends that they could find real Romanian smoked meat in a restaurant on Boulevard Saint-Laurent, and so they did.

They were tourists for a day, and such a day passes very quickly. In the evening, full of meat and new experience, they found their way along Sainte-Catherine Street to the Forum. They were laughing, and Nicolae and Veronica could not seem to keep their hands off each other. It was as Ionescu had suggested. They were in the new life. Without money, without a home, without even the promise of a job, they were nevertheless very happy people. Such a sight was the Forum, with its crowds of people outside, its boys selling programs and men in scarves selling tickets in the street. It seemed impossible that this thing, this hockey game, just a normal part of life in Montreal would be theirs for the evening.

And then Nicolae saw Ionescu, winking at him from behind a scarf. The invisible man, no longer so invisible to Nicolae after their formal introduction. He was pacing the street outside the Forum, yelling in near-perfect French, selling tickets to anyone who was interested. The tickets he had given Nicolae and his family were his bread. Ionescu yelled through his scarf at passersby, tempting them with tickets, and Nicolae could tell he was smiling broadly at the sight of him. He imagined the same scene from where Ionescu was standing. This little family who had looked so small and frightened in the morning, now smiling and full of food.

Feeling immense gratitude, Nicolae did the only thing he could think of to do. He took a hand from his pocket and sent a peace sign through the air to Ionescu. It was the sign only Nicolae's very good friends would use to acknowledge each other on the streets in Bucharest. It meant, we know each other. We are the same. Ionescu must have watched Nicolae make this sign hundreds of time in Bucharest, but only for friends. Nicolae could see only his eyes that evening, but he felt sure it made Ionescu very happy to see this sign directed at him.

"That was Dragos's introduction to this game he has become so good at," Nicolae says through more cigar smoke.

Tony has slowed his searching now, the alcohol and exhaustion beginning to gain advantage. In a darkened corridor, he finds a wooden bench and sprawls across it, defeated. He feels an ominous nausea building in his gut.

"It's interesting, yes, to consider how we travelled from that first ever hockey game, to this moment here? How what begins in foreignness and uncertainty can become the very centre of things."

Ionescu had not given them the best seats, but on that night what did they know? They were very high up in the building, and the chairs very narrow and hard. It was all a bit tight and uncomfortable, but with a perfect view of the playing surface. Veronica twisted in her seat, observing the crowd, looking to see what it meant to live in Montreal, what other people wore, how they spoke to each other. Before that night, the only other hockey matches Nicolae had seen were at outdoor rinks. He was accustomed to watching the game standing up in the freezing cold and trying to see over the heads of all those in front of him. But in the Forum the upper stands fell away so steeply, all the ice was revealed to them despite the crowd. It turned the match into a sort of board game, and for the first time, that night, Nicolae began to understand the subtler skills of the sport. He could watch the movement of the puck from player to player, adjusting to set defences like pieces on a chessboard. The strategies became apparent.

On that evening, Canadian hockey began to resemble Romanian soccer, and Nicolae understood its attraction. The speed and individual skills of the players. The pace of the game, and of course, the almost unrestrained violence. It all reminded him of the soccer one sees in Bucharest, and also a little of his own game, the handball he played as a youth. Rough and fast. Beautiful.

Fifteen

"Tony, don't worry. It is all just part of the ceremony." The drunken bridegroom, Dragos Petrescu, clapped a sweaty hand on the back of Tony's neck.

"I would have warned you about it, but I didn't think they would take the Cup as well. Usually, it is just the bride that goes, stolen off to somewhere, and I must now pay a ransom to get her back. It is just a tradition. It is to show how much I am devoted to her, how much I love her. It is the last test of my loyalty before I am allowed to have her for life. I think they simply couldn't stop themselves; it was too funny for them to take the Cup as well, so now we both have to pay a ransom to get our women back. Do not worry about the Cup. They are keeping it safe, as safe as they will keep Irina. They must keep it safe, or there would be no point in ransoming it."

Dragos sits with Tony at the head table, trying to reassure him, a roomful of wedding guests smiling into their faces. Tony has just returned from the bathroom where he has thrown up his dinner, several glasses of champagne and several more of țuică. His eyes ache and a shaking in his hands has become uncontrollable. His bow tie is gone, his jacket is off and he has rolled his shirtsleeves to the elbow. He wants to begin yelling, but doesn't. He thinks about games and weddings and the polite disasters people visit upon each other in the name of fun.

He remembers the moment a crowd of wedding guests closed around him, blocking his view of the Cup. He remembers being too drunk and too intent on winning a kiss to care about anything else. He recalls the moment he stopped caring about the Cup. He is a little in awe of how he stopped paying attention, and in awe of the empty podium. Tony stands and walks to the red-curtained doorway of the room's far closet. Petrescu follows him, laughing here and there and berating the crowd in Romanian. Tony reaches behind the curtain and drags a black case into the light. He can tell the Cup is not inside by the weight of the case, but he opens it anyway, checking its compartments, making sure of his white gloves and the silks he uses for cleaning the trophy. When Petrescu reaches out to pat his shoulder, Tony blocks his arm away. There is violence in his defence. Petrescu stumbles backwards.

"It's easy for you," Tony says to the drunken champion. "You have everything."

In the Forum that night, there was the noise of the crowd, the music from the loudspeakers, a great warm energy throughout the building, much excitement. And when one looked to the ice, there was such light and colour. The Montreal players in white and red and the New York players in blue. Dragos Petrescu-Nicolae sat at the very edge of his small seat there, very high up in the Forum. He was watching the skaters do their circles in preparation for the start of the game. He was consuming this sight, this spectacle, like it was fresh water and he had been so terribly thirsty for such a long time. He had his hands on the seat and he was lifting his little bum up and letting it drop again. He was bouncing in his seat, unable to control the excitement that was pulsing in his small body. His excitement was a beautiful thing for his parents to watch. For over a year they had worried in the night that they were damaging our child with their decisions. But here was real happiness again; in fact, a happiness like they had never seen in him.

The game began and Dragos watched the movements of the puck and the shifting of the players. He learned the basics of the game within the first ten minutes and soon he was explaining the action to his parents.

"They must stop now because that player there, number 29, crossed that blue line before the black disc."

"Watch now as those three players leave the ice and three other players come on. It will happen very quickly. See, now. They don't stop the game to change like in football, they just change."

"They will bring the disc all the way back and drop it to the ice near the goal, I think because it crossed all the lines without another player touching it."

On their way home from this game, the family stopped in a drugstore on Sainte-Catherine's and Dragos asked for a notebook and some coloured pencils. In the morning there were drawings of the Montreal team sweater, hockey sticks and skates, and a detailed diagram of a hockey rink, perfectly accurate with all the lines and circles. Dragos had pencilled in the positions of players for all the goals that were scored the previous night.

"Yes, Tony, I have everything now. You are right."

Tony feels his stomach twist again.

"People ask me," Petrescu continues, "how it is possible a boy who had never even seen a hockey rink until he was eleven could develop into such a good player. It is simple and anyone can do it. You can do this thing yourself Tony, no matter what you say about your height."

Diana has wandered away from the crowd and is standing beside her cousin now. She looks with amused concern into Tony's face.

"Tony, just make it so that hockey is the only thing to make you forget your greatest sadness. Allow hockey to replace the love and everyday affections of grandparents and the only real home you have ever known, to stand in for a language that slips away from you every day in a thousand unstoppable ways. Anyone can win your precious cup if they do just this one thing."

Sixteen

"You must begin to think about this more clearly," Diana insists.

Outside the hall, the night has turned chill, summer heat disappearing in the forest air. Tony is being pushed along the narrow street by the gentle persuasion of Diana's two arms. The roads of the village are empty and every house he can see is black and lifeless. The only movement, the only heat is in the hall he has just left. He turns to face the building, to scan for lit windows, for secret rooms where the Cup might be. Shouts and music flow through the open front doors.

Dragos Petrescu had been carried from his chair and thrown into the dance floor. The band started into a brisk polka and one by one the women of the village made their way into the middle of the floor to claim their ransom. His payments continue.

"It was me who told them to take your cup. I was angry. I didn't think it would have such an effect on you." She pushes him by his arm, fights his inertia and starts him walking in slow circles around a courtyard.

"I don't understand, are you a man or a little child who has lost his toy?"

JOHN DEGEN

"I've told you. It's my job."

"A job does this to a man? Tell me Tony, do you live where Dragos lives? Do you live in Florida when it is cold and Montreal when it is warm?"

"I live in Toronto, cold and warm. I live where I was born. Like most of the people here."

"It's too bad. If you lived in Florida when it is cold and Montreal when it is warm, I would consider marrying you and coming to live such a life. You kiss very well. A husband, I think, must kiss very well."

Tony turns his face from Diana and pats for gum in his pockets. He regrets the vomiting.

"You would marry a man so quickly, after two kisses?"

"Yes, two kisses are enough, I think. And besides, you forget I was sitting on your lap for the second kiss. I know more about you than most women do, I think."

Diana leads Tony on a turn through the village. The sounds of Dragos's dancing ransom follow them through the darkness. She walks him through a beet field and out across a meadow to the church. Beside the church, there is a public well. She pumps fresh water into a waiting wooden bucket and hands Tony a scooped wooden spoon.

"Wash your mouth out completely. Gargle with this water and then spit it out. I don't want to be tasting your stomach if I have to kiss you again."

Tony ignores the spoon and grabs at the cold water with both hands, spilling it over his face and the front of his shirt. His teeth ring from the cold. He feels his head begin to clear. Diana stands to the side, smiling, appraising.

"This is what a man looks like. Fresh, awake, ready for any activity. Not whining and sobbing about some lost thing,

218

some nothing. Look at me. I lost a kiss in a game of back-gammon, and I did not throw up, though I might have."

Diana runs her hand across Tony's forehead, straightening the wet hair across his brow.

"You play backgammon well, for a Canadian," she says, flicking droplets from his cheeks.

"You know this game, this backgammon? It was a game of Roman emperors and generals. You think of chess as the game of war, but it is really just the game of strategy. Strategy is a necessary part of war, and so excellent players of chess may in fact be excellent wartime strategists, but even the greatest strategists have been defeated in war. Why? Because of the dice. Chess does not depend on the whim of dice, and therefore does not contain that most essential elements of war. Unpredictability. Fate. Stupid luck."

His shirt soaked, Tony begins to feel the cold of the forest air. He draws closer to Diana, pulling her warmth to him.

"How does a brilliant strategist like Napoleon fail to complete his vision of a continent under his cloak? He thinks only of the position of pieces on a board and has no thought for the rolling of the dice. In the dice are the Russian winter; in the dice are burnt livestock and destroyed crops; in the dice are his own advancing age and madness.

"Backgammon is the real game of war because it is possible to lose at the table even when you are the far superior player. It is possible for the dice to decide you need to be brought low, and when the dice decides such a thing, you are brought low. Roman emperors and generals understood better the whims of war, and this is why they were fascinated by backgammon. They wanted the dice to decide against them, knowing eventually it would decide *for* them as well. We are all Romans in that way, waiting to have favour returned to our lives. Sometimes, it does not return. For my great uncle Stefan, who died here in this village during the war, favour did not return."

Diana pushes harder on Tony's shoulders, walking him further into the village. Her voice continues, echoing against wooden buildings and out into the dark forest.

The village of Ilisesti is not much of a village. There are two roads: one that travels generally to the east or west, and one that intersects, travelling generally to the north and south. The north-south road is made of earth. Every year the town sprays it with oil to keep down the dust. The east-west road has been covered in asphalt by the regional government, to encourage tourism to the historic monasteries of Bucovina. Buses from Suceava travel this road, but they almost never stop in the village, continuing on to the larger villages containing the medieval monasteries famous for their fantastically painted churches.

There are one or two small inns on the main road. Some villagers have talked about building a restaurant for tourists, but worry they are too close to Suceava to convince anyone to stop. The tourists will have eaten before boarding the bus and by the time they get to Ilisesti they will not be hungry enough to stop for food. And food is all they have to offer. The village has been populated by farmers since before anyone can remember. Farmers have wonderful food, but if someone doesn't want food, there is little point in it being wonderful. Not hungry is not hungry.

The villagers of Ilisesti have been conquered by the Turks,

by the Hungarians, by the Russians several times, and by the Germans. They are a people who wish to stay where they are and farm the same land they have farmed for too many generations to count. That is the history they wish for themselves. One generation after the next, farming the same fields and raising the same animals.

When the country went fascist, a prison was built several miles from the village and young Communists were transported from Bucharest to spend the war behind its walls. It was a working prison, a farming institution where the young idealists were set to work growing vegetables for their German captors. Throughout the growing seasons they worked in the vegetable fields, producing potatoes and cabbages for German soldiers, and they themselves were fed a diet of little more than boiled cornmeal.

The Nazis took food from the villagers as well, as one would expect during an occupation. But always the local farmers managed to have enough for the occupiers and for their own families as well. If the Germans took three pigs from a farmer in one year, he kept two hidden in the cellar beneath the barn. Everyone in Ilisesti kept a secret cellar, and shared out the food among neighbours and friends.

Secret slaughters were carried out in these earth-lined, underground rooms—the squeals and screams of the dying animals drowned out by drunken singing—and the meat transported by night from village house to village house. If one house had extra meat, they would exchange it for some milk from another house, or for some țuică from yet another neighbour, and in this way the people of the village sustained each other under occupation. They had less than at other times, and it was difficult, but never desperate.

It was the young Communists in prison who ate the corn meal every night, and worked all day growing food they would not taste. Their signatures had appeared on paper, so the cornmeal was theirs.

In 1944, after years of occupation, the Nazis were still in control of the region, but it was certain they wouldn't be for much longer. The Russians were pushing the lines ever closer. The German soldiers spent much of their time studying maps of the routes leading back toward Germany, and in the evenings both the soldiers and the villagers would listen to the voices of Soviet propagandists broadcasting in increasing strength on an increasing number of radio frequencies. The Russians counselled patience, advised the Romanian peasantry that soon their comrades would arrive to liberate them from the Nazis.

The German garrison slowly depleted itself until all that was left were a few small rear-guard panzer units and the division of prison guards who, no one doubted, were to make sure no Communist prisoners were left alive to join with their liberators. One evening, a group of these few remaining German soldiers, a tank crew, blasted Ilisesti's old stone water tower to rubble and arranged the debris in the central intersection, blocking both roads as they crossed in the middle of the village. Their work completed, the soldiers retreated to the village tavern to drink, gamble and spend another nervous night waiting for the order to retreat.

There were seven village men in the tavern when the soldiers entered. By the time the Germans had ordered their drinks and sat down to begin playing each other at table, only three villagers remained. There was little luck to be

had around soldiers at that time, so in the initial disturbance of their entrance to the room, four villagers, their
hands fluttering up around their eyes, managed to slip out
of the tavern and make their way home along the darkened
streets. The old tavern owner and his middle-aged son had
nowhere else to go. They stayed to serve the soldiers and
suffer whatever fate waited them. The only other villager to
stay was a small, strong man named Stefan.

Stefan lived in the centre of the village in a tiny house,
and grew beets in a field adjacent to the water tower, now
destroyed. He owned the lumber mill at the edge of the
forest. Stefan's hands milled all of the wood used for the
fences and barns of Ilisesti, and all the wood was cut from
the village's own forest. Though a smart man, Stefan had
a weakness for alcohol, for the țuică he made himself in a
shack beside his mill. It was Stefan's țuică that most of the
village drank at the tavern.

A month before this night, Stefan's wife had died giving
birth to a son. He was in misery, and had been drunk already
several hours before the soldiers walked through the door.
He sat in the corner of the tavern, hunched over a backgammon board and a bottle of his own țuică.

The presence of the Germans in town was more misery
to Stefan, as they forced him to work longer days in the mill
to supply lumber for their own purposes. Stefan made it a
habit to regularly express his hatred for the Nazis, but only
under his breath and never within their hearing, even when
drunk. He was an intelligent man who understood the reality of life under occupation. But as the war dragged on, it
became apparent to everyone in the village that, even when
the Germans were defeated, Ilisesti would not be rid of idiot

masters. Hearing the Soviet broadcasts and anticipating a seemingly unending trouble, Stefan became less careful.

In the tavern that evening, drinking țuică followed by beer and then more țuică, and playing backgammon with the owner's son, Marian, Stefan had watched the soldiers enter. Against his own good judgment about such situations, he had decided to stay. He stared darkly at the three young men in their combat uniforms, his expression so ugly Marian hissed at him to leave while he still could. But Stefan would not leave as long as there was backgammon to be played.

"My great-uncle Stefan was a genius at the table." Diana walks Tony to the central intersection, a winding paved road interrupted by dirt. The remnant foundation stones of the old water tower sprouted tall weeds by the roadside. Tony feels controlled, manipulated. He enjoys the feeling.

When the dice were with him, Stefan could not be beaten, and on this night the dice were with him. With the German soldiers watching, he beat Marian eight games to two in a match for fifteen. It was a destruction. The entire time they played, Stefan drank țuică followed by beer and then more țuică; and the entire time they played, Stefan was being watched by these three panzer soldiers. They watched him and marvelled out loud at his luck with the dice, as though luck is all a Romanian needs to play the game. When the match against Marian was at an end, of course one of the soldiers offered to play Stefan.

It was not wise to say no to a German soldier without

very good reason. Even through his drunkenness, Stefan was aware of the danger of his situation and of the even greater danger awaiting him when he accepted the offer. As unwise as it was to play, it was certainly less wise still to beat a German soldier at backgammon, or any game for that matter.

It was difficult for Stefan to lose when the dice were with him. Such was his skill at the game that he could have found a creative way to lose without it looking like he was giving the game to the soldier. But he had been in the tavern all evening, and was just drunk enough from țuică followed by beer and then more țuică to lose this part of his skill. Contributing also to the moment was Stefan's great sadness, a certain mood of hopelessness, a despair that he would never again be his own man in a tavern without soldiers from some foreign country watching his every move.

Stefan agreed to play the soldier a match of fifteen, and the wager was set at one bottle of țuică. For Stefan, this was a meaningless wager, just something to make the game decisive. The winner would get the țuică, and the loser would pay for it. It would have been very easy for Stefan to lose this bet since he would hardly feel the loss of one small bottle of his own țuică. With the tavern owner and his son Marian watching, Stefan began the match in a manner certain to lead to his loss. He dropped the first two games slyly, leaving pieces uncovered and then reacting in horror when the soldier rolled the dice, to make sure the capture was not missed. But as the match progressed, and both men continued drinking, something changed. To the horror of the tavern-keepers, Stefan slipped back into his normal style of play. He had forgotten who his opponent was. He began to play again like the champion he was and, eventually, won the match eight games to five. Not so humiliating a match record for the soldier, but still a loss at the hand of a Romanian peasant.

Realizing he had made a mistake, Stefan opened the bottle of țuică and poured out large glasses for himself and the three soldiers, smiling and apologizing for the dice. The soldiers smiled and accepted the free drinks, but were not so easily distracted. Another of the soldiers now wanted to play Stefan. This young man, drunk and sick to death of fearing an imminent Soviet attack, intended to win back the honour of the German Army on the table. Marian complained about the time, about the need to close up the tavern and go home to a wife and children, but the soldiers refused to be moved.

Another hard-fought match of fifteen began, and with the games tied at five apiece, Stefan did something unimaginable. He offered to raise the bet. The soldiers laughed and slapped Stefan on the back. They had decided to like this courageous little Romanian with the incredible luck at dice. But Marian and his father sank into despair. They knew that for Stefan to raise the bet at this point meant he had decided he would win, and that could only mean trouble for everyone in the room.

The Germans were satisfied with their position in this match. Their wins, through Stefan's skill at deception, had seemed decisive, and Stefan had made sure his own wins were the result of blind luck. To anyone who did not know Stefan, it would have seemed the dice were on the side of the Germans, and so when Stefan offered to make it more interesting, the Germans assumed he was bluffing, desperately trying to make them back away from the match. They asked him what he had to offer.

In the distillery shed at the back of his lumber mill, Stefan had just completed bottling over three hundred new litres of țuică from that year's plums. He made it known to the Germans he was willing to wager the entire three hundred if they would put up something of equal value. The soldiers laughed. They were far from their homes. What did they have to wager with? Stefan had no interest in their German Army money, and anyway it is doubtful they would have had enough between them to cover the cost of three hundred litres of țuică.

It was Stefan who smiled then. He didn't want their money. If Stefan won, he said in his best, most formal and polite German, the soldiers would agree to retreat from Ilisesti, when the time came, on horses that Stefan himself would supply. Stefan would end up with their Panzer tank, the pride of the German infantry.

Marian could stand it no longer. At the mention of the tank he jumped from his seat behind the small bar and rushed to the gaming table. He swore at Stefan in Romanian and in the same sentence was politely conciliatory to the Germans in their own language. Obviously, this fool had been drinking too much țuică. Obviously he would never try to insult the great German army with such a foolish joke. If they would end the tournament now he, Marian, would see to it himself that Stefan delivered to them as much țuică as they could take with them, when he had slept off his idiocy, when he was not such an embarrassment to the Romanian people.

But the Germans would not hear it. The mention of the tank reminded them where they were, reminded them of the distance to their own homes and of the possibility that Stalin's troops were at that moment plotting how they were to be killed. Their tank was everything to them. It was the reason they were now a target for barbarian Russians, and it was the only thing that could save them from those same barbarians. At the mention of their battle home, all three soldiers began to nervously finger their side arm holsters. Stefan kept his eyes on their eyes. Somewhere deep within his drunkenness he recognized the line he had crossed. He smiled at the soldiers. They smiled at him.

Stefan had Marian bring another bottle of ţuică from behind the bar, and all the glasses were refilled. The match continued, Stefan playing for a German panzer tank, and the soldiers playing for a year's supply of the best ţuică in the country. But now, with the stakes as high as they could go, it was apparent Stefan would not allow a loss. He wanted to take the tank from these men. He had begun to feel he was fighting a war with the table, that perhaps his success at the table would mean success for his village once and for all against these and any future invaders. Stefan played a heroic final three games, beating the Germans in a humiliation, three games to nil. With the final roll of the dice, he slapped his palm on the board and shouted, "The panzer belongs to Ilisesti."

Refilling the glasses yet again, he toasted the soldiers. He toasted Germany. He toasted the factory and the factory workers who had made his fantastic tank. The soldiers remained silent throughout all of Stefan's drunken, victorious toasts. When Stefan looked around the room to share his victory with the village, he discovered that he was alone with his gambling partners. Marian and his father had slipped out the back door of the tavern and were hurrying through the dark fields. Stefan's tank sat in the town square, directly in front of his house where it had often been seen, its gun trained on the road into town from the forested hills of Bucovina.

There was no witness to Stefan's final moments that night. Marian claims to have seen Stefan and the three soldiers stumbling up Ilisesti's main road very drunk, singing German army songs. The men were arm in arm as though friends for life. There is no witness for what happened, but the entire village is aware of what they found the next day. Stefan lay in front of his tank, his face in the dirt of the road, a hole in the back of his head. The three soldiers sat against the side of Stefan's house in the centre of the village, drinking his țuică.

They sat with their Lugers drawn and told of how they had played yet another match after leaving the tavern, won back their tank and the three hundred bottles, and that Stefan had then attacked in a rage, trying to sabotage the panzer and shouting insults about Germany. They had not wanted to shoot him, but as members of the great German army they had no choice.

For the people of Ilisesti, it was an anxious, dangerous morning. The soldiers were still very drunk and in a blood rage from senseless killing. The villagers worked hard to make the killers comfortable again, to draw them back to humanity so no one else would be lost. They cleared Stefan's body from the roadway and congratulated the drunken men on both their win and the completion of their duty. The women of the village brought the soldiers breakfast and made sure to keep their țuică glasses full. Finally, overcome by their long night and many bottles of liquor, the Germans collapsed into sleep where they sat, crumpled against the house of the man they had murdered.

That is the last anyone ever saw of those men, or their precious panzer tank. The tank and the three murderous soldiers disappeared that morning. Other soldiers from their division swept the village before the final retreat but nothing was found. They searched through every house, looked through every barn for the tank. They burned down Stefan's lumber mill trying to intimidate someone into talking, but the villagers were unmoved by their story. The three soldiers had become very drunk one night in the tavern and had talked openly to some of the townspeople about deserting. They had asked for help from the villagers, who had refused, for the villagers believed in the German cause. The soldiers became violent, breaking into the distillery for more țuică, killing Stefan in the process. Then they boarded their panzer and drove out of the village into the forest, toward the advancing Soviet army.

Tank tracks in the dirt road supported their claim. This was the story on the lips of every citizen of Ilisesti, and though the Germans searched for three days, they could find no trace of the tank or their soldiers.

"A division of Nazis could not find the tank." Diana laughs, pointing up the roadway to the squat lumber mill built decades before to replace the one destroyed by Germany. "Stalin's glorious army found no panzer when they liberated Ilisesti. The panzer is still hidden in the village. There are pieces of it here and pieces of it there. Ilisesti won that tank in an honest game at the table, and they will never give it up.

"You think you can find one little silver cup in this dark village?" Diana slaps Tony lightly on both cheeks and brushes her lips against his. "You must begin to think about this more clearly."

Diana curls herself closer into Tony, pulling his arm over her shoulder and taking his hand in hers.

"Now, of course, I will be kissing you again. *If* you win back your cup. And only if you win back your cup."

"Where is the Cup?"

"More clearly, Tony. Are you a champion?"

"But you know what I have to do to get it back? Is it dancing?"

"Dancing is for grooms. Are you a groom?"

"No."

"Then something else."

When they re-enter the reception hall, there is no more music. The bride, Irina, has been returned to the celebration and she attends to an exhausted Dragos Petrescu, who is collapsed against the stage steps, his shirt open. He takes small sips from a cup of water in his new wife's hand. Tables and chairs have been moved, and the small backgammon table now sits in the centre of what had been the dance floor. Petrescu's new grandfather, Andrei, sits at the board across from an empty chair. As usual, everyone in the room is smiling at Tony. They cheer when they see Diana wrapped around him. Tony decides he hates the smiling, and the cheering even more.

"Ah," yells the exhausted bridegroom, "I recognize the look in his eye. I have seen this look in the locker room.

This is the look of a man who will not leave here without the Cup. If he has to kill us all, he will take that cup, and whatever else he wants, back with him to Canada."

When Tony is seated at the game board, Diana leans in to Tony's ear.

"Remember, he is not an old man. He is your opponent—your enemy."

Seventeen

Autumn is just days away. Tony stands beside his car and counts trees in the chill evening air. Skate-high on the sixth trunk from the road he finds the nail and the cottage key dangling from it. He straightens up and pictures Stan doing the same, always alone, an old man walking the gravel path from his car to his lakeside cabin, tired after some long flight from Europe, glad to finally be home.

"Thanks, Stan," he says to the cedars. "You really should have had a family, old man, someone with your blood to leave this to. But better me then some other asshole, am I right? I guess I deserve it."

He skirts the sagging building and walks first to the shore. The sun is well past the western trees and he is facing east. Lake Simcoe stretches out calm into purple blackness, spotted here and there with lights from the far shore. The lighthouse on Big Bay Point glows out suddenly and then fades, glows and fades. Tony stands in the darkness, counting the rhythm of the slowly turning light. A triple-decked paddlewheel chugs by far out on the lake. Tony hears the sounds of soft jazz bouncing in off the water, a saxophone and stand-up bass, laughter and shuffling feet.

The sign by the road had said *Coop*, the final *e* and *r* of Stan's last name lost to weather, or maybe never painted there in the first place. The sign above the threshold reads *Reward*. The door catches a bit on buckled floorboards. With its opening it releases the moist scent of a building rotting slowly into the muddy lakeside.

Tony palms the wall for the light switch, feels a moth brush his face in anticipation of the flare. The cabin walls are lined with shelves. Light bounces back at Tony from every angle. On the shelves sit hundreds of shot glasses, souvenirs of every hockey-playing country in the world, of every hockey team in every year since 1952. The dust on them is thin, barely there, but Tony picks up the cloth Stan has left folded over his chair and begins to wipe glasses, looking at their logos.

"This is as far as I go, Stan," he says. "I like it just fine, but it doesn't do for me what it did for you. I think instead I'll fill this house with some voices."

He scans the room with his eyes, looking for anything that doesn't reflect back to him the image of himself in an armlock with someone else's triumph.

"Diana will be landing in about two weeks, Stan. And she will kick my ass if she sees this place looking like this. Until then, maybe I'll start by getting a radio in here."

He nudges at the arm of Stan's one comfortable chair with his shoe.

"And maybe I'll do something to get that smell out of here."

On the lake, a lone powerboat slices past, its engine a dull hiss like the slow deflation of an air mattress.

Acknowledgements

Thanks to Miki, Andrei, Gino, Vasile, Peggy, Julius and Valentin for wonderful drunken stories. Thanks to Georgiana for reading first and getting all the accents right. Thanks to Chris Chambers and Tim Elliott for hockey. Thanks to Julia for long discussion over martinis.

I want to especially thank the people at Toronto's Gibraltar Point artists retreat centre (Susan, Claudia, Robert, everyone) for October 2001, a terrible, turbulent month during which the first draft of this novel was completed. More whiskey, please.

Thanks to Eva Blank for a fine first edit; to Silas White for wanting it and making it better; and to all at Nightwood Editions.

Finally, thanks to Jonathan Bennett. A good friend, though distant. Look Jonathan, it's a book.